She wanted roses, champagne and love

Prudence felt her cheeks burn. "Why don't you like me?" she asked. It became suddenly important that Haso should tell her whether he liked her or not.

"And if I ask you the same question, do I get a truthful answer?" he asked in return. "I think not. I suspect that neither of us is quite ready to answer that."

He smiled at her, and this time it wasn't even faintly mocking, but gentle and kind, so that she smiled back. "I expect you're right. It's called agreeing to differ."

He lifted a finger to a hovering waiter. "Let's drink to it." Champagne—Prudence sipped cautiously. Haso had offered an olive branch of sorts, and she must accept it gratefully.

Betty Neels is well-known for her romances set in the Netherlands, which is hardly surprising. She married a Dutchman and spent the first twelve years of their marriage in Holland and working as a nurse. Today she and her husband make their home in a small ancient stone cottage in England's West Country, but they return to Holland often. She loves to explore tiny villages and tour privately owned homes there in order to lend an air of authenticity to the background of her books.

Books by Betty Neels

HARLEQUIN ROMANCE

2787—A GIRL NAMED ROSE
2808—TWO WEEKS TO REMEMBER
2824—THE SECRET POOL
2855—STORMY SPRINGTIME
2874—OFF WITH THE OLD LOVE
2891—THE DOUBTFUL MARRIAGE
2914—A GENTLE AWAKENING
2933—THE COURSE OF TRUE LOVE
2956—WHEN TWO PATHS MEET

Paradise for Two

Betty Neels

Harlequin Books

TORONTO • NEW YORK • LONDON
AMSTERDAM • PARIS • SYDNEY • HAMBURG
STOCKHOLM • ATHENS • TOKYO • MILAN

Original hardcover edition published in 1988
by Mills & Boon Limited

ISBN 0-373-03004-5

Harlequin Romance first edition September 1989

CHAPTER ONE

THERE were two people in the room, facing each other across the breakfast-table—a small, elderly lady with iron-grey hair and very blue eyes in a pleasantly wrinkled face, and opposite her a girl with a charming face framed by curling russet hair and large hazel eyes, fringed by long, curling lashes.

'It's a splendid opportunity,' observed the elderly lady in a coaxing voice, 'and you would be doing a kindness—after all, Mrs Wesley is your godmother.'

Her companion frowned, her dark brows drawn together quite fiercely. She said in a no-nonsense way, 'Aunt Maud, I've only just left one job, and that was because I wanted a change—I've set my heart on that Ward Sister's post in Scotland,' she added as an afterthought. 'Besides, there's Walter...'

'Has he proposed again?' asked her aunt with interest.

'Well, yes...'

'You've accepted him?'

The girl smiled at the eagerness in her companion's voice. 'It's a funny thing, Aunt Maud, but I can't...perhaps it's because we've known each other for a long time and the gilt's worn off the gingerbread, or perhaps it's because Walter thinks I'm extravagant.'

'Well, you are, dear,' her aunt spoke mildly.

'I like clothes,' said her niece simply. 'Besides, it's difficult to find things to fit me. Everyone except me is size eight or ten.'

She stood up, and indeed she was nowhere near either of those sizes. She was a big girl, tall and splendidly built, her long legs clothed in elderly slacks topped by an outsize jersey.

Her aunt studied her thoughtfully. 'You won't marry Walter?' She sighed. 'Prudence, he would make a good husband . . .'

The girl frowned again. 'I don't want a good husband, I want to be swept off my feet, plied with champagne and roses and jewels—I'd quite like to be serenaded, too.' She glanced down at her magnificent person. 'But you can see for yourself, dear Aunt, that it would need a giant of a man with muscles of iron to get me off the ground. Shall I tell Ellen to come in and clear the table? I'm going for that job, I shall apply for it and post the letter this morning.'

Her aunt got up, too. 'Very well, dear. At your age I would have been delighted at the chance to travel abroad and see something of the world, but I dare say you know your own mind best. Your godmother will be disappointed.'

Her niece crossed the room and gave her a hug. 'Dearest Aunt, I have travelled a bit, you know, when Father and Mother were alive——' She paused a moment, and then went on steadily, 'They always took me with them. True, I've not been to Holland, but I don't suppose it's much different from England. Mrs Wesley will be able to find someone only too eager to go with her.'

Her aunt agreed meekly. It was barely half an hour later, as she sat in the sitting-room making out a shopping list, that Ellen announced a visitor.

Miss Rendell put down her pen and got up with every sign of pleasure. 'My dear Beatrix, how providential! I've been sitting here wondering if I should telephone you. Dear Prudence is even now applying for a post in Scotland, but perhaps you might dissuade her? She has no real reason for refusing to go with you to Holland, you know—indeed, she's very fond of you, and a complete change might check her restlessness.' She added vaguely, 'She wants to be swept off her feet.'

'And I know the very man to do it,' declared Mrs Wesley. She sat down. 'Let me have a try.'

Prudence, nibbling her pen and frowning over her application form, listened to Ellen's request that she should join her aunt downstairs with some impatience. The Vicar, she supposed, wanting someone to take a stall at the church bazaar, or old Mrs Vine from the Manor bent on getting Prudence to fill a gap at her dinner-table. Prudence, who had made her home with her aunt in the small Somerset village ever since her parents had died in a car crash, knew everyone who lived there, just as they knew her, and when she went to London to train as a nurse she still returned whenever she had leave. She loved the place and liked the people living there, from crusty old Colonel Quist living in solitary state in one wing of the vast house at the end of the village to Mrs Legg, who owned the village stores and ran the Post Office besides. She loved her aunt too, and the nice old house which had become her home, but she loved her work as well; she had spent the last six years in London, first training as a nurse and then taking over a surgical ward at the hospital where she had trained. It was on her twenty-fifth birthday, a month or so previously, that she had decided she needed a move right away from London before she got into a rut from which so many of her older colleagues either could not or would not escape. Scotland would do nicely; she would be really on her own there and it would be a challenge, finding her feet in a strange hospital and making new friends. She let her thoughts wander as she went downstairs. Perhaps she would meet the man of her dreams—a vague image, but she was sure she would know him if they met.

She hadn't expected to see her delightful godmother sitting with her aunt. She crossed the room and kissed the proffered cheek. Mrs Wesley was a formidable lady, not very tall but possessed of a well-corseted stoutness, a handsome face and a slightly overbearing manner. Prudence was very fond of her and said warmly, 'How nice to see you, Aunt Beatrix. I thought you were in London.'

'I'm staying there, my dear, but I've been the guest of Mrs Vine for a day or so, and I thought I'd call and see you both before I go back.'

'Oh—you mean to Holland? But you aren't going to return there to live, are you?'

'Certainly not, but my sister is ill—did your aunt not tell you? She has had a heart attack and needs great care, so I shall go to her and do what I can. I had hoped...' Mrs Wesley paused and heaved a shuddering sigh. 'But I expect we shall manage. In a few weeks I dare say she'll be stronger. It's a pity I've been told by my own doctor that I must take things quietly for a few months, but at such a time one doesn't think of oneself.'

'Why, Aunt Beatrix, what's wrong?' Prudence felt quite shaken; she couldn't remember her godmother being anything but in the best of health.

'Diabetes, of all silly things, my dear. I spent a few days at a nursing home while they decided what I couldn't eat and explained that tiresome insulin to me. I'm not yet stabilised, they tell me, but when that's corrected I need only take tablets.'

'You're having injections?'

'At the moment, yes. So tiresome, as I have to arrange for someone to come and give them to me—the district nurse here has been most kind...' She gave Prudence a quick look. 'That was why I'd suggested that you might like to accompany me to Holland, but of course, you young people must lead your own lives...'

Prudence shifted uneasily in her chair. She was being got at, and since she was a kind-hearted girl she could see nothing for it but to accept her godmother's invitation; the idea of Aunt Beatrix wandering around suffering from a condition she didn't fully understand, even in her own native country, wasn't to be entertained for one moment. She mentally tore up the letter she had just written to the hospital in Scotland, reflecting ruefully that here was one young person who was being thwarted from doing as she wished...

'When do you go?' she asked, and saw the pleased smiles on her companions' faces. 'I had intended to apply for a job in Edinburgh, but I'll see if they might have a vacancy at a later date.'

'Dear child!' Aunt Maud addressed her magnificently proportioned niece with no awareness of inappropriateness. 'Your dear godmother will be safe with you, and I dare say this hospital will be only too glad to offer you a job later on.'

Prudence smiled at her kindly; Aunt Maud, having lived her life in sheltered security, had no idea of the harsh world outside it and there was no point in disillusioning her. No hospital was going to wait while an applicant for a job waltzed off to Europe before taking up her job.

'How long do you intend to stay in Holland?' she asked.

'Oh, well—a month, no longer, by that time my sister should be well again, should she not?' Mrs Wesley added, 'She's in hospital, but if all is well she should be going home very shortly. I thought I might go next week.'

Prudence remembered without much regret that Walter had invited her to an exhibition of paintings on either Tuesday or Wednesday of the following week. He had told her rather importantly that it depended on whether he could get away from his desk; he was a junior executive in a firm of stockbrokers and took his work seriously; he also fancied himself as something of an expert on modern art. Prudence, who liked paintings to look like something she could recognise, had done her best to go along with his views, without much success.

'We shall fly,' observed her godmother, 'and naturally we shall be met at Schiphol and driven to Dornwier. Whether we shall remain there or accompany my sister on a holiday in order that she may recuperate from her illness, I don't as yet know.'

'You're sure your own doctor has no objections to you travelling, Aunt Beatrix?'

'Oh, yes, he quite saw my point of view.' Which was Aunt Beatrix's way of saying she had browbeaten the poor man into agreeing with her.

'Do you want me to meet you in London,' asked Prudence, 'or at the airport?'

'Perhaps you would come to my flat the day before we leave? Then we can travel to Heathrow together. Shall we say Tuesday of next week—provided I can get a flight then. I dare say you may have one or two things to see to before you leave.'

Clothes, thought Prudence and then, as a guilty afterthought, Walter. He would be annoyed, he didn't believe in young women being too independent. A woman's place, he had told Prudence on many occasions, was in the home.

Which was all very well, she had pointed out, but whereabouts in the home? Lying at ease on a chaise longue in the drawing-room, covered in jewels and pure silk, would be nice... Walter had no sense of humour; he had told her, in his measured tones, not to be foolish. It struck her suddenly that she didn't love him, never had, and that this invitation from her godmother presented her with an opportunity to make Walter understand that once and for all she really did not want to marry him. They had known each other for years now, and she wasn't sure when they had drifted into the idea of marriage. Certainly he had shown no overwhelming desire to make her his wife; on the other hand, she had been expected to tag along with him whenever she was at home, and in the village at least they were considered to be engaged.

She said now, 'If you'll let me know when you want me to come, Aunt Beatrix, I'll be there. There's nothing of importance to keep me here.'

She thought guiltily that Walter would be very annoyed to be designated as nothing of importance.

Ellen came in with coffee and the next half-hour was pleasantly taken up by Aunt Beatrix's plans; she had obviously got everything organised to suit herself, and Prudence wondered just how she would have reacted if she hadn't got her way. Aunt Maud was looking pleased with herself, too; Prudence looked at her two elderly companions with real affection, and when her godmother got up to go, bade her a warm goodbye.

'Tot ziens,' said Aunt Beatrix, who occasionally broke into her native tongue.

Prudence replied cheerfully, 'And tot ziens to you, Aunt Beatrix, though I'm not quite sure what that means! I must try and learn some Dutch while I'm staying with you.'

Walter called in that evening on his way home from his office in Taunton. His greeting of, 'Hello, old girl,' did nothing to make her change her mind about going away.

He sat down in the chair he always used and began at once to go into details about an argument he had had with one of the partners that day. Prudence sat opposite him, listening with half an ear while she took the chance to study him carefully. He was an inch or two shorter than she was and already showing a tendency to put on weight, but he was good-looking and, when he chose, could be an entertaining companion with charming manners. Only, over the years, the charm and the manners weren't much in evidence—not with her at any rate. She said suddenly, cutting through his monologue, 'Walter, when did you last look at me—I mean, really look?'

He gave her stare of astonishment. 'Look at you? Well, I see you several times a week when you're here, don't I? Why should I look at you? Have you changed your hair-style or lost weight or something?'

'I don't need to lose weight,' she said coldly. 'I sometimes feel, Walter, like your daily newspaper or the old coat you keep behind the back door in case it rains...'

He gave an uneasy laugh. 'My dear girl, what's got into you? You're talking nonsense. It's a good thing you're going to this new job, you've been too long at that hospital of yours in London.'

'You've asked me to marry you several times.'

'Yes, well—there's time enough for you to make up your mind about that, in the meantime you need to be occupied.'

'You don't want to sweep me off my feet? Rush off with me and get married?'

She felt sorry for him, because he was quite out of his depth; stockbrokers didn't like to be rushed.

'Certainly not; marriage is a serious undertaking.'

Prudence nodded. 'Yes, it is. Walter, I don't want to marry you. I'm sorry if it puts you out—I mean, you expected me to marry you when it was convenient, didn't you?'

'I say, old girl, that's a funny way of putting it!'

'But it's true.' She got up and wandered over to the window. 'I'm going to Holland for some weeks to stay with an aunt who's ill.'

'You haven't any aunts in Holland.' She heard the tolerant amusement in his voice.

'Courtesy aunts, one of them is my godmother and I'm fond of her. I think it would be a good idea if we parted, Walter—we can stay good friends if you want that, but don't expect me to change my mind. I really will not marry you.'

He had got to his feet, too. 'Suits me. You're a nice girl, Prudence, but you like your own way too much—men like a degree of meekness in a woman, especially in their wives.'

'I'll remember that.' Her eyes, large, brown-flecked with tawny spots, thickly fringed, flashed sudden anger. 'I hope you find a suitably meek girl willing to marry you, Walter.'

He said seriously, 'Oh, I have no doubts that I shall.'

He looked so smug that she itched to throw something at him, especially when he added prosily, 'But I doubt if you'll—what did you say?—find a man to sweep you off your feet. No hard feelings, Prudence?'

'None at all, Walter.' She watched him go without a pang, but deep inside her she was conscious of panic; she was, after all, twenty-five years old and, although she had never lacked for men friends, she had never wanted to marry any of them. Perhaps she would never meet a man she could love and marry...

Aunt Maud bustling in to ask if Walter was staying to supper dispelled her thoughts. Prudence wandered across the room and shook up a number of cushions which were perfectly all right as they were. 'What would you say if I told you that I'm not going to marry Walter? We've parted quite definitely.'

Aunt Maud said: 'Well, dear, since you ask me, I feel bound to say I feel profound relief. Walter is an estimable young man, but in ten years' time he'll be pompous and bossy. None the less, he would be a good husband if one considers the material things of life—he would never allow his wife to be shabby, and the children would go to the right schools.' Aunt Maud sighed deeply. 'But no romance, that's something I think you might not be able to do without.'

Prudence flung her arms wide. 'Oh, you're so right, Aunt Maud, but where am I to find romance? And for the next few weeks there'll be no chance to find it at all—Aunt Beatrix is a darling, but she hasn't any family other than her sister, has she? And I feel in my bones that any doctors I may meet will be elderly and bald.'

Her aunt agreed placidly and kept her thoughts to herself.

There was a good deal to do during the next few days; according to Aunt Maud, Prudence's godmother came from a well-to-do family and her sister lived in some style.

'Somewhere in Friesland, isn't it?' asked Prudence, her pretty head on one side, critically examining a dress she wasn't sure she wanted to take with her. And, before her aunt could reply, 'Do you suppose it will be good weather there? I know it's May, but it's a good deal farther north actually than it is here.'

'A knitted suit?' suggested her aunt. 'And tops and skirts—you could take a couple of thinner dresses in case

it should really warm up.' She added casually, 'I should
put in a pretty dress for the evening, dear—your Aunt
Beatrix knows a number of people there, and you might
get asked out to dinner.'

Prudence thought it unlikely, but her aunt looked
wistful, so she packed a slim sheath of corn-coloured
silk, deceptively simple and very elegant, and a silk jersey
dress with long sleeves, a sweeping skirt and a square
neckline cut rather low. It was of indigo blue, an excellent foil for her hair. It would give the balding eld-
erlies a nice change from thermometers and stethoscopes.

Prudence drove herself up to London in her down-at-
heel little Fiat. She had friends at the hospital where she
had been working, and one of them, the junior in the
team of theatre Sisters, had agreed to garage the car at
her flat provided she might have the use of it, a plan
which suited Prudence very well. She left the car, took
out her luggage from its boot and hailed a taxi to take
her to her godmother's flat. It was in an Edwardian
building along the Embankment, very ornate out-
wardly, but a haven of quiet luxury once past its well-
guarded entrance. Prudence left her luggage with the hall
porter and took herself up to the first floor, to be ad-
mitted by her godmother's elderly maid, a dour, middle-
aged spinster with the unlikely name of Miss Pretty.

Prudence greeted her cheerfully, knowing that be-
neath the gloomy face there lurked a loyal, kind heart.
'The porter's bringing up the luggage, Pretty. Is Aunt
Beatrix in?'

'Waiting for you, Miss Prudence, and tea on the table.'

'Good, I could do with a cup. You are coming with
us, Pretty?'

'Madam couldn't manage without me,' said Pretty austerely. 'Not that I care for foreign parts myself, although it's quite nice where we're going. Her stern features relaxed slightly. 'Madam's that pleased that you'll be coming with her.'

'I'm looking forward to it,' declared Prudence, and added, 'Shall I go in? The drawing-room?'

Mrs Wesley offered a cheek to be kissed. 'Dear child, how nice you look! Sit down and let's have tea. I thought a quiet evening? We shall be leaving after breakfast. That good man Best will drive us to Heathrow.' Best carried on a hired car business from the mews behind the flats, and Aunt Beatrix would have no other.

'And at Schiphol?' prompted Prudence, sinking her splendid teeth into a scone.

'My sister is sending her car to meet us.' Mrs Wesley sipped her milkless tea and watched her goddaughter make a splendid meal. She said with a trace of envy, 'You can eat anything you like? You don't put on weight?'

'Not an ounce, and that's a blessing, since I'm what our Vicar calls a fine figure of a woman, which is a polite way of saying that I'm a big girl.'

Her godmother glanced down at her own ample proportions. 'You're tall enough to carry it,' she observed, 'and I flatter myself that I'm able to do the same.'

Prudence nodded a cheerful agreement and began on a cucumber sandwich.

They left the next morning, and Prudence, in the habit of throwing a few things into the back of the Fiat and driving away, was taken aback by her godmother's elaborate preparations for a journey which would take less

than half a day. For a start, the amount of luggage was
sufficient for a stay of several months, and comprised
a number of old-fashioned and very bulky hatboxes, an
awkwardly shaped leather case which Pretty clung to as
though her very life depended on doing so, a large trunk
which required two men to lift it, and a variety of suit-
cases. Prudence, with one case and an overnight bag,
began to wonder if she had packed enough clothes to
compete with such a vast wardrobe. It took some
considerable time to hoist everything into the boot, and
even then poor Pretty, sitting in front with Best, had a
conglomeration of umbrellas, travelling rugs and the
awkward box, as well as her own modest luggage. The
sum of money to pay on excess baggage would be
considerable—something which of course Aunt Beatrix,
with a more than adequate supply of the world's riches,
could ignore.

Prudence admired her almost regal indifference to the
hustle and bustle of Heathrow when they reached it; it
was left to herself, Pretty and Best to organise porters,
find the right desk and settle the question of excess
baggage, although to give Aunt Beatrix her due, she paid
up without a murmur when asked to do so before making
her stately progress towards the departure gate.
Prudence, a law-abiding girl, had always thought one
should arrive, as asked, one hour before the plane de-
parted, but this was something her godmother had either
overlooked or considered unnecessary. They bade Best
goodbye and made their way through the security check
and into the area set aside for outgoing passengers. It
was almost empty and they were among the last on
board. First class, of course, and Aunt Beatrix, in the

nicest possible way, wanting her seat changed, a cushion
for her head and the promise of a glass of brandy as
soon as they were airborne. She disliked air travel, she
informed the stewardess in a ringing voice, and expressed the hope that the Captain was an experienced
man. Having been reassured about this and having had
her seat-belt fastened, she gave Prudence, sitting beside
her, her handbag to hold, arranged herself comfortably
and went to sleep. The stewardess, coming presently with
the brandy, gave it to Prudence instead. She drank it,
since it was a pity to waste it, and ordered one for Pretty,
who sipped it delicately, making it last for almost the
whole of their flight.

Mrs Wesley woke as the plane started its descent to
Schiphol, observed that the flight had been a pleasant
one, and warned Prudence, who had the tickets, to be
sure she didn't lose them.

The rather slow business of getting from the plane to
the airport exit went without a hitch; with the luggage
piled high on three trolleys, they arrived in the open air
to find a uniformed chauffeur waiting for them.

He greeted Mrs Wesley with great politeness, ac-
knowledged Prudence's polite good morning with a
bowed head and grinned at Pretty. The car waiting for
them was a very large Mercedes into which Aunt Beatrix
stepped and settled herself comfortably, leaving everyone
else to load in the luggage, with Prudence giving advice
which only Pretty understood and the porters taking no
notice of anyone at all. But at length everything was
stowed away to the chauffeur's satisfaction; he held the
door politely for Prudence to get in beside her god-

mother, saw Pretty into the seat beside him, and drove off.

'We go around Amsterdam,' explained Aunt Beatrix, 'and join the motorway going north. We shall cross the Afsluitdijk into Friesland, and from there we drive across Friesland very nearly to Groningen Province. I think you'll find the country pleasant enough; there should be a map in the pocket beside you, dear, so you can see exactly where you are. I shall compose myself and take a nap—I find travelling very fatiguing.'

Prudence somehow choked back a giggle, and presently opened the map.

She hadn't realised quite how small Holland was. They were on the Afsluitdijk within two hours, speeding towards the distant coastline of Friesland; they must be almost there. Aunt Maud had warned her that she might expect to find her hostess's home somewhat larger than her own. 'I visited there once, a long time ago,' Aunt Maud had said, 'and I remember I was rather impressed.'

The car swept on, skirting Franeker and Leeuwarden, racing along the main road towards Groningen. What was more, Prudence had seen very few country houses, but numerous villages, each with its church, offering useful landmarks in the rolling countryside, and any number of large prosperous farms. She was wondering just where they would end up when the chauffeur turned the car on to a narrow brick road, and within minutes they had left the modern world behind them. There were trees ahead of them and a glimpse of red roofs, and, as though Mrs Wesley had secreted an alarm clock about her person, she opened her eyes, sat up straight, and said in a satisfied voice, 'Ah, we're arriving at last,' just

as though she had been awake all the time. She said
something to the chauffeur in Dutch and he replied at
some length as they slowed through a small village; a
pretty place surrounded by trees and overseen by a red
brick church in its centre. The road was cobbled now
and the car slowed to a walking pace as it rounded the
centre of the village and took a narrow road on the other
side.

'A lake?' asked Prudence. 'How delightful!' She was
still craning her neck to get a better view when the car
was driven between stone pillars and along a curved
drive, thickly bordered by shrubs and trees. It was quite
short and ended in a wide sweep before a large, square
house with a gabled roof, a very large front door reached
by double steps and orderly rows of large windows. There
was a formal flower garden facing it beyond the sweep,
and an assortment of trees in a semicircle around it.
Prudence, getting out of the car, decided that it was
rather nice in a massive, simple way. It might lack the
mellow red brick beauty of Aunt Maud's home, but it
had charm of its own, standing solidly in all the
splendour of its white walls in the May sunshine.

The procession, led by Mrs Wesley with Prudence
behind her and tailed by Pretty and the chauffeur,
carrying the first of the baggage, mounted the steps, to
be welcomed by a stout man with cropped white hair
and bright blue eyes. He made what Prudence supposed
to be a speech of welcome, and stood aside to allow them
into a vestibule which in turn opened into an oval entrance hall. Very grand, reflected Prudence, with pillars
supporting an elaborate plaster ceiling and some truly
hideous large vases arranged in the broad niches around

the walls. The floor was black and white marble and cold to the feet.

There were numerous doors, and the stout man opened one and ushered them into a large room furnished in the style of the Second Empire, with heavy brocade curtains at its windows and a vast carpet on its polished floor. Aunt Beatrix took off her gloves, asked Pretty to see that the luggage was brought in and taken to their rooms, and sat down in a massive armchair. 'Wim will let my sister's maid know that we have arrived,' she observed, 'but first we'll have coffee. I suggest that while I'm seeing my sister you might like to stroll through the gardens for half an hour.'

Prudence agreed cheerfully. 'And when do you take your insulin?' she wanted to know.

'Ah, yes, I mustn't forget that, must I, my dear? And my diet...'

'You have it with you? Shall I go and see someone about it? It's very important.'

Her godmother was searching through her handbag. 'I have it here, but I shall need to translate it. How many grammes are there in an ounce?'

They worked out a lunch diet while they drank their coffee, and gave the result to Wim, and Mrs Wesley said comfortably, 'I shall leave you to arrange dinner for me, dear; if you'll write it out I can translate it... I dare say you're clever enough to ring the changes.'

Prudence agreed placidly, concealing the fact that she was a surgical nurse and had always loathed diabetics anyway. 'You'd like me to see to your insulin, too?' she asked.

Her godmother nodded. 'But of course, Prudence.'

A small, stout, apple-cheeked woman came presently to take Mrs Wesley to her sister. Before she went, she suggested once again that Prudence should go into the garden around the house. 'My sister will want to meet you,' she concluded, 'but first we must have a chat.'

When she had gone, Prudence wandered over to the doors opening on to the terrace behind the house and went outside. The gardens were a picture of neatness and orderliness. Tulips stood in rows, masses of them, with clumps of wallflowers and forget-me-nots between them. All very formal and Dutch, she reflected, and made her way past the side of the house, down a narrow path and through a small wooden gate. The path meandered here, between shrubs she couldn't name, and there were clumps of wild flowers, ground ivy and the last of a splendid carpet of bluebells. She turned a corner and ran full tilt into a man digging. He straightened up, and said something in Dutch and turned to look at her. He was tall and heavily built, so that she felt quite dwarfed beside him. She had read somewhere that the people of Friesland and Groningen were massively built, and this man was certainly proof of that; he was handsome, too, with lint-fair hair, cut unfashionably short, bright blue eyes, a disdainful nose and a firm mouth. The gardener, she assumed, and murmured a polite good day.

He stood leaning on his spade, inspecting her so that after a moment she frowned at him. And when he grinned and spoke to her in Dutch she said sharply, 'Don't stare like that! What a pity I can't speak Dutch.' And at his slow smile she flushed pinkly and turned on her heel. So silly to get riled, she told herself, walking away with great dignity. He hadn't said a word—or at least, none that she could understand.

She went back into the house and presently she was taken upstairs to a vast bedroom and introduced to Aunt Beatrix's sister—Mevrouw ter Brons Huizinga, a rather more stately version of Aunt Beatrix, if that were possible, sitting up in bed against a pile of very large linen-covered pillows. Despite her stateliness, she looked ill, and Prudence eyed her with some uneasiness. She enquired tentatively after her hostess's health, and was reassured to hear that her doctor visited her daily and was quite satisfied with her progress. 'He should be here any minute,' declared Mevrouw ter Brons Huizinga, and, exactly on cue, there was a tap on the door and he came into the room. The gardener, no less.

CHAPTER TWO

AUNT BEATRIX swam forward and enveloped him in her vast embrace. 'My dear boy, how delightful to see you again and to know that you are taking such good care of your aunt! We've only just arrived...' She had spoken in English and turned to glance at Prudence, standing with her mouth deplorably half-open and with a heightened colour. 'Prudence, this is my nephew—at least, he's my sister's nephew; Haso ter Brons Huizinga. Haso, this is Prudence Makepeace who has kindly come with me so that there's someone to look after me. She's a nurse.'

Prudence offered a hand and nodded coldly. He didn't look like a gardener any more; he had rolled down his shirt sleeves and put on a beautifully tailored jacket, and his hands looked as though he had never done a day's work, let alone dig a garden. He held her hand firmly and didn't let it go. 'Ah, yes, Prudence, I've heard a good deal about you.'

A remark which annoyed her. She said sharply, 'You could have said who you were!'

He raised his eyebrows. 'Why?'

She was stumped for an answer.

He said thoughtfully, 'You aren't my idea of a Prudence.'

'Indeed?' She had managed to get her hand back at last.

He put his handsome head on one side, contemplating her. 'Small and pink and white and clinging.'

He shook his head and she said tartly, 'What a disappointment I must be, Doctor—er—ter Brons Huizinga, not that your opinion interests me...'

'Oh, dear, we've started off on the wrong foot, haven't we?'

Aunt Beatrix had gone over to her sister's bed, but now she paused in what she was saying and turned to look at them. She said in her rather loud voice, 'Getting to know each other? That's right, you young people will have a lot in common.'

'Young?' murmured Prudence unforgivably, and looked pointedly at his hair—there was quite a lot of grey in it. She was annoyed when he laughed. 'Well, I dare say you must seem young to my aunt,' she added kindly.

He didn't answer, but strolled over to the bed. 'Aunt Emma, I should like to take a look at you as I'm here. Would you like your maid here? Or better still, could Prudence help you?'

Aunt Beatrix got up. 'Why, of course she will. I shall go to my room until luncheon. Before you go, Haso, will you arrange a diet for me? I have a letter from Dr Lockett in London. Insulin, you know,' she added vaguely.

He opened the door for her. 'Of course, Aunt Beatrix.' He added something in Dutch to make her laugh and then returned to the bedside.

He was very much the doctor now. For Prudence's benefit he spoke English, although from time to time he lapsed into his own language while he talked to his aunt. When he had finished his examination he sat down on the side of her bed. 'You're doing very nicely, and now you're in your own house you'll do even better. You may get up tomorrow for a short time: I'm sure you're in capable hands.' He glanced at Prudence, who looked rather taken aback; she had been prepared to keep an eye on Aunt Beatrix, but now here was a second elderly lady to worry about.

'Aunt Emma has a splendid maid, quite able to cope if you would prefer that.' His eyes were on her face, but she refused to look at him. Instead she turned a smiling look towards the bed's occupant.

'I shall enjoy looking after you,' she said firmly.

'That's settled, then—we'd better deal with this diet, had we not?' He glanced at his watch. 'I have ten minutes to spare. Perhaps you could get the diet sheets and instructions about the insulin and bring them down to the small sitting-room.'

Prudence hadn't the least idea where the small sitting-room might be—indeed, she reflected, neither did she know where her room was. Presumably someone would tell her in their own good time. She wished Mevrouw ter Brons Huizinga a temporary goodbye and went through the door he was holding open. She had swept past him rather grandly, only to stop short in the corridor outside. She had not the least idea where to go.

'Aunt Beatrix will be in her usual room—go to the end of this corridor and turn left, it's the first door on your right.' He caught her arm. 'It will be quicker if I show you. Do you know where your room is?'

'No, but I hope someone will tell me before bedtime.'

He stopped, and she perforce stopped with him. 'Not much of a welcome. You should have been warned that

the Aunts take it for granted that their minds are read
and their wishes carried out without the necessity of them
needing to put them into words.' He walked on again,
turned a corner and nodded towards a door. 'There's
Aunt Beatrix's room. The sitting-room is on the left at
the bottom of the staircase.'

Aunt Beatrix was resting on her bed watching Pretty
unpack. 'There you are, dear child. Luncheon will be in
twenty minutes—in the family dining-room. Do you want
something?'

Prudence collected the diet sheets, the insulin and the
doctor's letter and went downstairs. Dr ter Brons
Huizinga came to the door as she reached the last stair.
'In here, Prudence—you don't mind if I call you
Prudence?'

He didn't wait for her to answer but started reading
the letter, having first invited her to sit down. The room
was rather pleasant, although she found the furniture
rather heavy. But it was beautifully cared for, and the
ornaments and silver scattered around were museum
pieces. She glanced up and found the doctor's eyes upon
her. He smiled suddenly, and just for a moment she liked
him, but the smile went as quickly as it had come, and
he turned away to a chair opposite hers.

'There couldn't be a worse diabetic than Aunt Beatrix,'
he observed in his faintly accented English. 'Keeping her
to a diet won't be too bad, but once she's stabilised and
off injections, the chances of her remembering to take
her pills are slight. However, we'll do our best.'

He got out his pen and spread the diet sheet on his
knee and began to write it out in Dutch. Prudence sat
and looked at him; he really was very good-looking, and

far too sure of himself, almost arrogant. She wondered where he lived, and as he put his pen away she asked, 'Do you live here, too?'

'No. Now, the insulin...'

Prudence blushed at the snub, although she supposed she had deserved it. She listened to his instructions, received back the diet sheet and his own written instructions as well as the doctor's letter and the insulin, and got up to go.

'Presumably you're on the telephone if I should need you?'

'Indeed I am.' He opened the door and then shut it again before she could reach it. 'Tell me, did you expect there to be a nurse here to look after Aunt Emma?'

She raised her eyes to his. 'Well, yes, I did—I mean, Aunt Beatrix asked me to come along too because she was a little uncertain about the diabetes.'

'The naughty old thing,' he observed softly. 'I'll get a nurse from Leeuwarden; she can be here by this evening.'

'No, please don't do that, Doctor. I wouldn't know what to do with myself all day, and there'll be very little to do for your aunt.'

'Coals of fire, Prudence?'

'Pooh,' said Prudence roundly, 'such rubbish! Perhaps you'll be good enough to tell me what you want done.' She went on loftily, 'I've been in charge of a twenty-bedded ward for some years, so I'm quite capable of looking after both your aunts.'

'I have no doubt of it. I'll stay to lunch, and afterwards we can decide what's best for the pair of them.'

He opened the door and she went past him into the hall, not knowing where to go next. 'In here,' he said, and opened another door. 'Time for a drink before we lunch.'

'I should like to go to my room.'

He glanced at his watch. 'I'll get someone to take you up; come back here and I'll have some sherry poured for you.' He added carelessly, 'Don't be too long.'

A remark calculated to convince Prudence that it would take her at least fifteen minutes to see to her face and do her hair to her liking. And who did he think he was, giving orders in his aunt's house? She followed a cheerful young girl up the staircase and down a corridor at the end of which was the pleasant room she was shown into, with windows overlooking the grounds at the back of the house. Her clothes were already unpacked, she noticed, and there were towels and soap arranged in the adjoining bathroom. She sat down before the dressing-table mirror and peered at her reflection. Her face needed very little done to it; she dabbed on some powder, applied lipstick and took down her hair and did it up again, not because it needed it, but because the doctor had told her not to be long. Really, she admonished her reflection, it wouldn't do at all; she would have to see quite a lot of him at least for the next few days, and she must at least pretend to like him. Which reminded her that it would be a step in the right direction if she didn't keep him waiting too long.

If he had noticed that Prudence had been at least twice as long as he had expected, he gave no sign, and presently Aunt Beatrix joined them and they crossed the hall to the dining-room, a forbidding apartment with a massive sideboard weighed down with quantities of silver and a table large enough to seat a dozen people. The meal was simple but elegantly served, and her companions carried on a conversation about nothing much, taking care to include her in it. They must be longing to lapse into their own tongue, she reflected, but neither of them gave a hint of wanting to do so, and when they had had their coffee the doctor invited her into a small room leading off the dining-room and asked her to sit down.

The next half-hour was spent in a résumé of Mevrouw ter Brons Huizinga's state of health, with a polite request for Prudence to keep an eye on her and call him if she was worried, and a somewhat detailed discussion about Aunt Beatrix. At the end of it he thanked her with cool politeness, begged her to say immediately if she found her responsibilities too heavy for her, observed that he would be in on the following day and wished her goodbye.

Prudence sat where she was for a little while, contemplating the next week or so. It was obvious to her that this was to be no ordinary visit. Aunt Beatrix, much as she loved her, had behaved quite ruthlessly, no doubt pleased with herself for having found someone to look after both herself and her sister. On the other hand, in all fairness, she was going to live in the lap of luxury, and possibly when she had found her feet there would be the chance to do some sightseeing. She allowed her thoughts to dwell on the delicious cheese soufflé which had been served at lunch, and decided that the pros more than outweighed the cons.

Both ladies snoozed in the afternoons; Prudence took herself into the gardens and explored. They were too formal for her liking, but since it was a warm afternoon she found them pleasant enough, and presently found a nice sheltered corner in the sun and curled up on the grass and went off to sleep.

'Sleeping Beauty?' asked a gently mocking voice which brought her wide awake, just for the moment quite scattered in her wits so that she blinked up at the doctor leaning over her.

'Oh, it's you again!' she declared crossly. 'I might have known!'

'Not Sleeping Beauty,' he observed blandly, 'just a cross girl. I came in on my way back from hospital to tell you that I shall be in Amsterdam tomorrow and probably for the next few days as well. I've left a telephone number on the hall table; my partner will come at once if you need anyone. He speaks English.' He turned on his heel. 'You hair's coming down,' he told her, and walked away towards the house.

She watched him go; never in her whole life had she met a man she disliked so much!

She went back to the house presently, but only when she had heard a car driving away. Aunt Beatrix was in the drawing-room, the tea-tray in front of her. 'Go and tidy yourself, my dear, and we'll have tea together. My sister is still sleeping. Haso has been here again—I expect you saw him.'

Prudence said that yes, she had, and she would only be two ticks tidying herself for tea, and sped away to her room. She got back to the drawing-room just in time to remove a large chocolate cake from Aunt Beatrix's vicinity.

'You're on a diet,' she reminded her. 'You must keep fit so that you can help Mevrouw ter Brons Huizinga . . .'

'You're quite right, dear. I think you might address my sister as Aunt Emma. We're to be together for some time, and I have always thought of you as my niece.'

Prudence thanked her nicely and eyed the chocolate cake; it seemed mean to have some when her companion was nibbling at a dry-looking biscuit. She would probably lose a lot of weight, she reflected gloomily, and gave herself another cup of tea with plenty of milk and sugar.

She spent an hour or so with Aunt Beatrix after tea, then went to see Aunt Emma. Aunt Emma's maid, Sieke, seemed pleased enough to have help in getting her mistress settled for the night, a by no means simple task, since Aunt Emma was a law unto herself, knowing better than anyone else and determined to have her own way at all costs. Sieke cast her a grateful look when at last they had the lady with her incongruous wishes nicely settled against her pillows with the promise of a light supper to buoy her up. They had not, of course, been able to talk together, Sieke had no English and Prudence had no Dutch, but they had had no need of words; it was apparent that Sieke was quite willing for Prudence to take over any nursing care necessary and felt no animosity about it.

Prudence went along to her own room, showered and changed into one of the pretty dresses Aunt Maud had advised her to pack. 'And a good thing too,' she muttered as she poked at her hair, 'if I'm to live up to the splendour of the dining-room.'

It was indeed splendid—white damask, shining silver and polished glass and a massive centrepiece which effectively blocked her view of Aunt Beatrix, resplendent in black velvet. Conversation, carried on in raised voice the length of the table, was concerned wholly with Aunt Beatrix's diet and her sister's health. Prudence managed to make a splendid meal before joining her godmother in the drawing-room for coffee, and then she sat listening to a somewhat rambling history of the family. 'Of course, your Aunt Emma married very well; her husband was a younger brother of Haso's father and they're a wealthy family. One wonders why the dear boy works so hard at being a doctor when he might be living quietly at his home.'

'Perhaps he likes being a doctor?' suggested Prudence mildly.

'Possibly. But his mother would like to see him married—there are several suitable young women...'

Not very interested, Prudence observed, 'Perhaps he's a confirmed bachelor. He's not young.'

Her godmother sighed and said reprovingly, 'A mere three and thirty, a splendid age at which to marry.'

Prudence longed to ask why, but decided not to.

Her godmother proceeded, 'There's no lack of young women who would be only too glad to marry him.'

'Oh, really?' said Prudence politely. 'Then why doesn't he? Marry, I mean?'

'You don't like him,' observed her godmother suddenly.

'I don't know him, Aunt Beatrix. How could I possibly dislike or like him after only a few minutes' conversation with him?'

'That is, of course, true,' conceded her godmother. 'You'll naturally get to know each other during the next week or so.'

An unnecessary exercise as far as Prudence was concerned.

The following day gave her a very good idea of what was to come. She awoke refreshed from a sound night's sleep to find her aunt's maid standing by her bed with early morning tea.

Her, 'Good morning, Pretty', was answered a little sourly.

'Well, good morning it may be for some,' declared Pretty, 'but I'm sure I don't know.'

'What's wrong?' asked Prudence; it couldn't be too dire, the house's inmates were barely awake.

'There's Madam, wanting rolls and butter and croissants with more butter and marmalade, with scrambled eggs and bacon, and sugar in her coffee...'

Prudence scrambled up higher against her pillows. 'That won't do. I'll come and see my aunt, Pretty—it's no good her having a diet if she's not going to keep to it. Don't you worry now, go and have your breakfast, if you like. I'll let you know what's happening.'

She got out of bed and flung on her gown, a gossamer affair of crêpe-de-Chine and lace which matched her nightie.

'That cost a pretty penny,' declared Pretty severely.

Prudence agreed readily. 'I like pretty things.' She smiled at Pretty and stuck her feet into satin slippers trimmed extravagantly with satin bows, then took herself out of the room to visit her aunt.

Mrs Wesley was sitting up in her bed sipping milkless tea in a discontented fashion, and it took all of ten minutes to coax her to have the breakfast she was allowed and not the one she wanted, but Prudence was used to dealing with recalcitrant patients, and presently she went away to dress and go downstairs for her own breakfast—the last peaceful minutes she was to have until lunch time, as it happened. Between them, Mrs Wesley and her sister kept her busy for the entire morning; their demands for this and that and the other were numerous, uttered with charm and a stately determination to have their own way. It was a relief to everyone when they consented to rest on their beds after lunch. Prudence tucked them up with soothing murmurs, waited until she heard their gentle snores, and escaped into the gardens. It was a splendid day, warm for the time of year. She found a pleasant seat in a quiet corner and opened her book.

It was obvious that each meal was going to be a battle of wills between herself and her godmother. Prudence reflected that it was a good thing that Mevrouw ter Brons Huizinga had a well-staffed household, devoted to her. There was to be no lack of help when Prudence was summoned to get that lady from her bed, an undertaking which took a great deal of time and almost all her patience. All in all, she thought as she got ready for bed that night, a busy day, and as far as she could see, all the other days would be the same.

They were, at least for the next three days, but by now she had a routine, frequently disrupted by the vagaries of the two elderly ladies, but none the less workable. Not speaking Dutch was a disadvantage, of course, but it was amazing what could be done with arm-waving and pointing.

The fourth day came and went and there was no sign of Haso, and although Prudence reminded herself that she disliked the man intensely, none the less, she wished he would come. It had been rather unfair, she reflected, giving way to a self-pity she seldom indulged in, that she had been left with the responsibility of the aunts. Of course, she could get his partner at any time, but that wasn't the same thing... She got into bed with something of a bounce and declared to the empty room, 'Well, I suppose he'll turn up sooner or later.'

Sooner, as it turned out.

She wakened to the sound of Pretty's urgent voice hissing at her.

'Miss Prudence, for heaven's sake, wake up—there's something wrong with Madam, and there you are snoring your head off!'

Prudence opened one eye. 'I never snore.'

Pretty gave her shoulder a little shake. 'Oh, do listen— you must listen! I know there's something wrong, Madam's lying there and I can't rouse her! I can't think why I went to see if she was all right, but she's not...'

Prudence was out of her bed, feeling around for her slippers with her feet.

'Hyperglycaemic coma,' she said, although she still wasn't quite awake.

Pretty said sharply, 'Call it anything you like, my Madam's ill.'

She was quite right; Mrs Wesley, as far as Prudence could judge, was in a diabetic coma, although they couldn't think of a reason for it. She had eaten her diet, every morsel, at dinner—Prudence herself had seen to that—and her insulin had been the correct dosage. She took a brief look at her godmother and went swiftly to the telephone.

It was Dr ter Brons Huizinga who answered her, and she didn't waste time with so much as a hello. 'Mrs Wesley—she's in a hyperglycaemic coma—deep, sighing breaths. I'm unable to rouse her at all...'

He cut her short. 'I'll be with you in fifteen minutes.'

Prudence went back to her godmother and then got out the insulin and syringe. 'And if you'd go down to the front door and let the doctor in, Pretty?'

He was as good as his word; she was bending over Mrs Wesley when he came into the room.

He didn't bother to greet her, his, 'Well, what has she been eating?' was uttered in a voice which, while not accusing, certainly held no warmth.

'Her normal diet. I had all my meals with her and I'm certain of that.'

He was examining the unconscious figure on the bed. 'Aunt Emma—dined in her bed?'

'Yes, of course. She only gets up for an hour or two in the afternoon.'

'She had a normal meal this evening?'

Prudence's eyes opened wide. 'Oh, my goodness! Aunt Beatrix went to sit with her...but that was after Pretty had taken the tray away. She had coffee...' She gave a small gasp. 'Some friends called to see her today and left a large box of chocolates.' She stared as his expression changed. 'You think...?'

'Let us assume that it's the chocolates.'

He had nothing more to say, but set about the business of dealing with his patient, an intravenous saline drip, soluble insulin given intravenously, following this with an even larger dose by injection, a blood sugar test and specimens taken for testing. He worked quietly, quickly and calmly, talking only when it was necessary, taking it for granted that Prudence knew what she was doing, too.

It was early morning, two hours later, before Mrs Wesley showed signs of coming out of her coma. An hour later, after a small injection of insulin and glucose to counterbalance its effect, she was completely conscious. Prudence heaved a relieved sigh and longed for a cup of tea, just as Pretty poked her head round the door in a cautious manner and hissed, 'Tea?'

It was Dr ter Brons Huizinga who answered her in a normal voice.

'A splendid idea, Pretty—and while you are getting it perhaps you, Prudence, would go and get a fruit drink for my aunt.

There was a beautiful dawn breaking as she went down to the kitchen; she fetched the drink, gave it to a remarkably subdued patient and then accepted a cup of tea from the tray Pretty had fetched.

'I'm going back home,' observed the doctor. 'I want two-hourly testing, and for the time being around thirty grams of carbohydrate four-hourly. I'll be back after morning surgery, but please phone if you're worried.'

Prudence looked at him with cold dislike, but said with deceptive meekness, 'Very well, Doctor. Presumably you'll arrange for someone to take over while I dress, eat breakfast and cast an eye over your other aunt?'

He said cordially, 'Most certainly, since you feel you can't cope.'

She said tartly, 'Don't be so unreasonable—of course I can cope, and you know it, but I doubt if you intend to take your surgery dressed as you are and with a bristly chin, too. So why should I spend the morning in a dressing-gown until you choose to do something about it?'

'It's a charming garment; for my part, you have no need to dress.'

Her dark eyes flashed with temper; she said with chilling civility, 'I suppose you can't help being rude!'

He looked as if he was going to laugh, but all he said was, 'If you could dress yourself and eat breakfast in half an hour, I'll stay—but not a moment longer.'

Prudence sniffed, 'How kind!' She cast a glance at Aunt Beatrix, lying with her eyes shut, looking more or less normal again, and whisked herself away.

Pretty, encountered on her way to her room, promised breakfast in ten minutes, and Prudence, with years of practice at dressing at speed in hospital, showered, donned a cotton top and a wide, flower-patterned skirt, tied her hair with a ribbon, and, since the ten minutes was up, left her face unmade-up before going down to the kitchen where the faithful Pretty was waiting with coffee and toast.

'Mevrouw's cook may be out of the top drawer, but she hasn't an idea how to cook a decent breakfast. All this bread and bits and pieces to put on it—give me bacon and eggs and a mushroom or two...'

Prudence, her teeth buried in her first slice of toast, agreed indistinctly. 'When in Rome, do as Rome does,' she added, and helped herself to a slice of cheese.

'Madam will be all right now?' asked Pretty anxiously.

'I believe so—we caught her in time. I do hope she won't do it again.'

She munched steadily for a few minutes, swallowed her coffee and got up. 'I'll take a quick peep at Aunt Emma. Will someone see to her breakfast?'

'Don't you worry, miss, there's help enough in this place. Has the doctor gone yet?'

'No, but he will the moment I get back to Aunt Beatrix.'

'Such a nice young man!' Pretty allowed her stern features to relax into a sentimental smile.

Prudence didn't think this remark worth answering. She thanked her companion for her breakfast and flew upstairs, two minutes in hand.

Aunt Emma was still snoring peacefully; she skimmed along the corridor and went into Aunt Beatrix's room.

'Ah, there you are.' Dr ter Brons Huizinga glanced at his watch, an observation which did nothing to improve her opinion of him, uttered as it was in a tone of pained patience.

'Half an hour exactly,' she pointed out. 'If you'd give me your instructions...?'

He did so, watched by his patient, lying back on her pillows now, with the drip taken down, looking almost normal again. 'Perhaps you would be good enough to fetch the notes I left by my aunt's bed when I last visited her?'

He watched her with a slightly sardonic expression while she bit back the desire to tell him he could fetch them for himself on his way downstairs. With a slightly heightened colour, she went out of the room and Aunt Beatrix remarked from her bed, 'You don't like each other?' She sounded so disappointed.

Haso was strolling about the room, his hands in his pockets. 'My dear Aunt—given the fact that we've both been out of our beds since about one o'clock this morning, and are in consequence a trifle edgy, I hardly think your observation applies.'

'Well, I do hope not. She's a sweet girl, and so sensible.' She studied his face. 'She's extremely pretty, Haso.'

'Indeed she is. Also not very biddable and a little too sharp in the tongue. Probably due, as I've already said, to having to get out of her bed so very early in the morning.'

'I'm very sorry... but the chocolates were most tempting.'

He smiled very kindly at her. 'I'm sure they were, only don't be tempted again. Be a good soul and keep to your diet, and in no time at all you'll be able to have all sorts of little extras. They make special chocolate for diabetics, you know.'

Mrs Wesley brightened. 'Oh, do they? Good. How is your Aunt Emma, my dear?'

'Doing very nicely. I'll go and see her now.' He kissed his aunt's cheek, nodded casually to Prudence, who had just returned, took his notes from her and went away, whistling cheerfully.

The day passed uneventfully; it was amazing how quickly Mrs Wesley recovered. By teatime she was sitting in her sister's room, exchanging somewhat exaggerated accounts of their illnesses. The doctor had been back again, pronounced himself satisfied as to their conditions, and gone again after a brief talk with Prudence. Very professional and standoffish he was too, she thought, watching his vast back disappearing down the staircase.

She wondered where he lived, but she hadn't liked to ask anyone, and certainly not him; she could imagine how he would look down his arrogant nose at her and tell her, in the most polite way possible, to mind her own business.

Mrs Wesley appeared to have learnt her lesson, and her sister was making steady progress; Prudence felt free to spend a little time on her own, exploring. The lake she had glimpsed on her arrival was close by; she found her way to it without much difficulty, circled it, poking her pretty nose into a boathouse on its near shore and then on the following afternoon wandering down to the village, where she bought postcards and stamps at the one shop; easily done by pointing to whatever she wanted and offering a handful of coins she had borrowed from her aunt. It had been foolish of her not to have thought of getting some Dutch money before she had left England; traveller's cheques were of no use at all.

The doctor called briefly on the following days. It was at the end of one of these visits that he surprised Prudence very much by suggesting that she might like to go to Leeuwarden. 'My aunts are well enough to leave to Pretty and Aunt Emma's maid for a few hours; you must wish to see a little of the country while you're here.'

She said baldly, 'I want to go to a bank and change my cheques. I had no idea that Aunt Emma lived so far away from a town...'

'Not far at all,' he corrected her. 'I'm going to Leeuwarden after lunch tomorrow. I'll give you a lift.'

'How kind. How do I get back?'

'I'll show you where to wait until I pick you up.' He was refusing to be nettled by her faintly cross voice.

She thanked him with cool politeness, and since he just stood there, looking at her and saying nothing, she felt compelled to make some sort of conversation.

'The lake is charming,' she commented, 'and I walked to the village—are there other villages close by?' She gave him an innocently questioning look in the hope that he might say where he lived.

His laconic 'several' was annoyingly unhelpful.

Her two patients behaved in an exemplary fashion. She helped get Aunt Emma out of her bed before lunch, had her own meal with Aunt Beatrix, an eagle eye on that diet, and then hurried away to change.

She was not dressing to impress the doctor, she assured her reflection as she got into a jersey three-piece in a flattering shade of pale green, thrust her feet into high-heeled, expensive shoes, found their matching handbag and, with a last look at her pleasing appearance, went downstairs.

Haso was in the hall, sitting on the edge of a console table, reading a newspaper and whistling cheerfully. He got up when he saw her, wished her good day and added blandly, 'Oh, charming—for my benefit, I hope?'

'Certainly not, pray disabuse yourself of any such idea.'

'Not an idea, just a faint hope. I thought it would be nice if we could cry truce for a couple of hours.'

Prudence said calmly, 'I'm quite prepared to be friendly, Dr ter Brons Huizinga...'

'Call me Haso, it's quicker. Good, let's go then.'

There was a dark grey Daimler outside on the sweep before the house. He opened her door and she settled herself comfortably, prepared to enjoy the drive.

She certainly did. Haso took a small country road to begin with, joined a quiet main road after a few miles and then went across country until they traversed the outskirts of Leeuwarden. The scenery was green and calm, with cows in the wide fields and every so often a canal cutting through the quiet landscape. The doctor was on his best behaviour; he discoursed at length about their surroundings in a serious voice which none the less gave Prudence the uneasy feeling that he was secretly amused. But he had cried truce for the afternoon, and she for her part was prepared to keep to that. She answered him when called upon to do so, and felt vague relief when they reached the outskirts of the town—a relief which turned to indignation when he observed silkily, 'Boring, isn't it, being on our best behaviour? Shall we agree to disagree when we feel like it?'

She swallowed her astonishment, but before she could decide what to say he had stopped the car in a quiet street.

'Out you get,' he told her. 'Turn left at the corner and
you'll find you're within yards of the centre of the town.
You'll see the Weigh House across the street—I'll be there
two hours from now. You can't get lost, the shops are
all close by and there are several banks where you can
change your cheques. *Tot ziens.*'

He had driven off before Prudence could frame a
reply. She hadn't known quite what to expect, but certainly she hadn't imagined she would be dumped off with
so little ceremony. She wasn't going to waste time over
him; she went to the corner, and sure enough it was
exactly as he had said.

She cashed her cheques, took a closer look at the
Weigh House and then strolled around the shops; there
were several small things she needed; it was rather fun
to pick them out for herself and compare the prices. She
spent quite a considerable time at a silversmiths, choosing
beautifully made coffee-spoons for Aunt Maud, and then
browsing around its counters. Indeed, it was pure chance
that she glanced at the clock and saw that it was five
minutes past the two hours she had been allowed.

The Weigh House wasn't far way; she could see the
Daimler parked nearby and approached it with some
trepidation; the doctor might be someone she didn't like,
but he was also a man to be reckoned with.

She braced herself for whatever he was going to say.

Nothing. He got out of the car, opened her door for
her and got back in only then, saying mildly, 'We'll have
tea, shall we? I telephoned the aunts—everything is quite
all right, so Pretty tells me. We'll go home—my mother
would like to meet you.' He spoilt it all by adding silkily,
'And I'm sure you're dying to know where I live.'

CHAPTER THREE

As FAR as Prudence could judge, they were going back the same way as they had come, but presently she realised that the narrow brick road they were on was turning north. She looked in vain for landmarks, but the fields all looked alike, with distant clumps of trees, all looking the same as each other.

'Confusing, isn't it?' commented the doctor. 'We're only a few kilometres from my aunt's house—there's a narrow lane a little farther ahead which leads to it. Those trees ahead of us hide Kollumwoude, where I live.'

The village proved to be pretty: red-roofed cottages, one or two villa-type houses, a shop or two and, brooding over the lot, a red-brick house of some size, encircled by a cobbled street. There were high wrought-iron gates half-way round it, standing open, and the doctor drove through them. 'Home,' he observed laconically.

Very nice, too, decided Prudence, taking in the house before them at the end of the short, straight drive. It was three storeys high, its windows set in three rows of three, with a round tower at each end, both of which had a pointed roof like a gnome's cap, as had the central building, and added to one side was another smaller wing with yet another tower. The windows were shuttered and the walls here and there were covered by a green creeper of some sort. The whole gave a pleasing appearance reminiscent of a fairytale castle. Only, it wasn't quite a castle, it looked too lived-in for that: there were curtains at its windows and orange window blinds over them. She said rather foolishly, 'Oh, is this where you live?'

'Yes.' He leaned over and undid her seat-belt, got out and opened the door for her and ushered her towards the door before them. Of solid wood, it had a fanlight above which was a small balcony, supported by two pillars. The door was opened by an elderly man just as they reached it, and when he stood aside for them to enter, the doctor spoke to him and he replied in a creaky voice. The doctor announced, 'This is Wigge—and that's a good old Friesian name—he looks after us all.'

Prudence shook hands and Wigge smiled at her and waved her into the hall beyond: square and lofty, with white walls, a beamed ceiling and any number of rather dark paintings hung upon the walls. There was a wide staircase to one side, rising to a gallery above, and several doors on either side of her, while beside the staircase she could see steps leading down to a door with leaded panes and, beyond that, a garden.

Rather to her disappointment, the doctor led her through the hall and out of the door on to a paved walk, bordered thickly by late spring flowers; it extended along the back of the house, ending at a small, arched doorway set in the high red-brick wall which enclosed the garden.

Prudence would have lingered here too if she had been given the chance, but she was urged towards the door which the doctor opened and invited her to go through. Here was another garden, enclosed in the same manner, its orderly beds filled with rows of vegetables, fruit bushes and the first shoots of a splendid potato crop.

There was a greenhouse running the length of one wall and the sound of music coming from it.

It was warm inside. Prudence, urged on by the doctor, began to walk along its length between pots of tomatoes which yielded a fine array of begonias and primulas and finally roses, not yet in flower.

The lady bending over a rosebush was undoubtedly the doctor's mother; as she straightened up, Prudence could see that she was tall, strongly built and good-looking still. Her hair was silver-gilt, pinned back in an old-fashioned bun, and her eyes were as blue as his. She smiled when she saw them, turned off the radio on the bench beside her and wiped her hands on the gardener's apron she was wearing.

'Haso—how nice! And you've brought Prudence with you.' She offered a hand. 'Of course, I've heard all about you from your godmother, and I'm so glad to meet you at last. We will go into the house and have tea—Haso, will you find Domus and tell him to finish these roses.'

She led the way out of the greenhouse, and Haso disappeared into a small path completely hedged in by shrubs.

'How do you like Friesland?' asked Mevrouw ter Brons Huizinga. 'Not that you will have had much chance to see anything of it, I dare say. Let us hope that Emma and Beatrix will recover their good health as speedily as possible.' She glanced at Prudence, walking serenely beside her. 'They are charming and I am very fond of them, but they have an independence of spirit—my husband had it also...'

Prudence couldn't think of anything to say other than a polite, 'Indeed?'

Her companion added drily, 'Haso is exactly like his father.'

Prudence wondered just what independence of spirit meant. Personally she thought it another way of saying that he was arrogant, sometimes rude. It wouldn't do to say so, of course; she murmured politely and followed her hostess into the house.

The hall looked just as grand from the garden door. They crossed its polished wood floor and entered a room opposite the staircase. It was large, high-ceilinged and lit by square windows with leaded glass and draped by heavy plum-coloured curtains. There was a magnificent carpet covering most of the floor, worn in places with constant wear over many years, and the William and Mary winged settee echoed the colour of the curtains as well as the muted blues and greens of the carpet in its tapestry cover. There were winged armchairs too, a vast display cabinet along one wall and still more paintings, mostly precious portraits. Prudence gazed about her frankly and her hostess asked, 'You like old furniture?'

'Very much. Aunt Maud has some nice Georgian pieces, but this is earlier. It reminds me of Mompesson House—that's in the Close at Salisbury...'

'Ah, yes—I have been there, and you are quite right, only I believe this house is older and somewhat larger. You must come soon and spend a day with me, and I will show you round.'

She motioned Prudence to sit in one of the armchairs and took one close by, turning to say to her son as he came into the room, 'You could bring Prudence over one day, couldn't you, Haso? In a few days' time, perhaps, once your aunts are recovered sufficiently.'

'Certainly, Mama, providing Prudence doesn't mind fitting in with my timetable.'

He looked across at her, smiling a little, waiting for her answer.

'Not in the least,' she said sedately, 'provided I'm free to do so.'

Wigge came in with the tea-tray then and the talk became general and then settled down to a mild discussion on gardening, Mevrouw ter Brons Huizinga's lifelong hobby.

'Haso has inherited my green fingers,' she observed happily. 'He usually finds time to potter for an hour or so at the weekend if he is free. He has done a great deal to improve Emma's garden—her gardener has no imagination at all.'

They had finished their tea when the doctor looked at his watch.

'I'll take you back on my way to Leeuwarden. I'll be back to change, Mama—I won't be in to dinner.' His mother looked a question and he went on smoothly, 'I'm taking Christabel out.'

So he had a girlfriend—even a fiancée?—and what a silly name the girl had, thought Prudence, saying her polite goodbyes, busy with a mental picture of the young lady in question: tall and blonde, if the Friesians she had met were anything to go by, cold blue eyes and regular features, and self-assured. Prudence, a good-natured girl, felt an unwonted dislike of her.

She was driven back to Aunt Emma's house briskly and with a scant attention to polite conversation. As she got out of the car, she said in a kindly voice which she guessed might annoy Haso, 'So kind of you to bring me back—was it your good deed for the day? I do hope you have a pleasant evening with your Christabel. She must be quite exceptional.'

She didn't wait for him to answer that, but raced into the house, where she encountered Pretty in the hall.

'What's the hurry, miss?' that lady enquired severely. 'Doctor brought you back, did he? All the more reason to linger, I'd have thought.'

'Linger? With him?' Prudence gave a strong shudder. 'Besides, he's in a hurry to spend the evening with his girl.'

'Got a girl, has he?' Pretty said, 'Hm,' and took herself off; here was a titbit of news which Madam wasn't going to relish. Pretty, a recipient of her mistress's confidences, knew quite well that she had been nurturing sentimental ideas about her goddaughter and her nephew.

Prudence, happily unaware of this, took herself off to her room as well, where she went to the window, to hang out of it and enjoy the gardens below while she allowed her irritation to evaporate. She wasn't a conceited girl, but people liked her, and several men of her acquaintance had wanted to marry her, Walter having been the most persistent. Although her heart hadn't been touched she had liked them all, even been a little fond of them, but none of them, she felt, were capable of sweeping her off her feet, regardless of whether she wanted to be swept or not.

She sighed heavily. In a week or two she would go back to Aunt Maud and start looking for a job, and if she didn't find one to her liking quite quickly she might even give up her romantic ideas and say yes to Walter.

At least he appeared fond of her; Dr ter Brons Huizinga didn't even like her, and, what was more, he made no attempt to hide his dislike.

She went to peer into the looking-glass on the dressing-table and poked at her bright hair. Perhaps he didn't like its colour. She studied the rest of her person; probably he liked slim-looking, delicate girls, and she was neither. It struck her suddenly that she was allowing him to occupy her thoughts far too much. She pulled a face at her reflection and went downstairs to find Aunt Beatrix.

That lady eyed her thoughtfully. 'You had a pleasant afternoon, dear? And you enjoyed tea at Haso's home? Dear Cordelia—his mother, you know—is the sweetest person. Wrapped up in her garden, of course, but it keeps her busy. I believe she still misses my brother-in-law, they were very close.'

Prudence sat down. 'I liked her. Has she other sons and daughters?'

'Three daughters, married and living—let me think— two of them in the Hague and the youngest in Groningen.' Mrs Wesley peered at Prudence over her glasses. 'All very happy, I believe. A pity Haso can't settle down too.'

'Perhaps he will—he's taking out someone called Christabel this evening.'

Mrs Wesley pursed her lips. 'The eldest van Bijl girl, good background—from *adel*, that's our aristocracy, you know—and very aware of it, too. By no means the partner for Haso.'

'Well, I suppose he'll decide that for himself.' Prudence sniffed. 'She sounds just right for him.'

'You speak as though you dislike him, dear.'

'Me? I don't care either way, Aunt Beatrix.' Being a fair-minded girl she added, 'He's a very good doctor.' She got up. 'I'll just run upstairs and take a look at Aunt Emma—temperature and so forth.'

Haso wasn't mentioned again that evening; they dined presently, Prudence feeling mean as she ate her sole, which was bathed in a delicious sauce and accompanied by croquette potatoes, courgettes in a cream sauce, and tomatoes with a forcemeat stuffing, while her aunt ate boiled fish, one potato and the courgettes without a sauce. She had prudently arranged for a larger flower arrangement to be placed between them, so that her godmother's eyes would be shielded somewhat from her companion's plate, which happily enough prevented her from doing more than glimpsing the trifle richly decorated with whipped cream which Wim, Aunt Emma's butler, offered her.

Aunt Beatrix, spooning up a tastefully arranged grapefruit, paused to say, 'I shall call on Cordelia—you shall drive me over, Prudence. We'll enjoy a pleasant chat. The grounds are delightful and I'm sure she will have no objection to you exploring them. Your Aunt Emma is very much better—I'm considering the idea of taking her on a short holiday as soon as Haso allows it. I should like to have you with us, of course...'

'Where to?' asked Prudence.

'I've always wished to visit the Channel Islands, and I believe Emma would like that. Not Jersey, it's too much of a holiday centre. Guernsey would be better.'

Prudence ate the rest of her trifle. 'Aunt Beatrix, I should really return home once Aunt Emma is better; I have to get a job.'

'I know, dear, of course you do.' Her godmother spoke with all the assurance of someone who had never lifted a finger to earn her own living all her life. 'But another week or so won't make much difference, will it?'

That it might actually make a difference to the contents of Prudence's pocket hadn't occurred to her. Prudence said non-committally, 'Well, let's see what the doctor says,' and Mrs Wesley, quite sure she would get her own way, agreed.

It was some days before they saw Haso again. His partner called, examined the two ladies, pronounced himself satisfied with the pair of them, cautioned Mrs Wesley not to eat anything she shouldn't, agreed with Prudence that since she appeared to be stabilised there was every chance of her having tablets instead of injections of insulin, warned her that Mevrouw ter Brons Huizinga shouldn't exert herself in any way, and took himself off with the remark that Haso was away and should she need any help she was to telephone him.

Prudence, having seen him off at the front door, went thoughtfully into the house. For a GP, Haso seemed to lead a very free life; she wondered about that and then told herself, rather reluctantly, that it was none of her business anyway. She didn't like him, she reminded herself.

All the same, when he arrived a couple of mornings later, she had to admit to herself that he wasn't a man to be ignored. It wasn't just his good looks and his size; it was ridiculous to suppose any such thing, but each time she saw him she had the feeling that they had known each other all their lives. Quite stupid, she reflected, greeting him with chilly politeness.

He didn't appear to notice that, his 'Hello' was casual and he wasted no time in small talk. 'Aunt Beatrix is ready for tablets?' He didn't wait for her to answer. 'I've brought them with me; start her off in the morning, will you? Keep an eye on her and do the usual testing—let me know at once if she backslides. I'll take a look at Aunt Emma. She should be well enough to be up and about for most of the day.'

He pronounced Aunt Emma remarkably fit and listened patiently to her plans to go on holiday. 'In a week or two, dear Haso, and I shall be quite safe, for Prudence is coming with us and she is such a good nurse. Beatrix thought Guernsey... It should be fairly quiet at this time of year—she knows of a good hotel.'

He said, 'I see no reason why you shouldn't go, my dear, since Prudence has kindly offered to go with you as your nurse.' He shot a quick look at her, standing on the other side of her aunt's chair. She returned it calmly, aware that he had, in some way she couldn't guess at, realised that she had offered no such thing.

As he prepared to go, he paused as they went down the staircase together. 'My mother would like to see you again. I understand from Aunt Beatrix that she wants you to drive her over one day.'

He gave her a quick glance and she said snappily, 'I can drive.'

He looked surprised. 'Well, so I had imagined. Will you come to lunch tomorrow? My mother and aunt will want to gossip, I dare say, so please feel free to roam around the gardens or explore the house. I doubt if I can get back until the late afternoon.'

Prudence thanked him pleasantly; he might not much like her, but he had been thoughtful...

They left the next morning in the small Fiat Wim had for his and the staff's use, Prudence having flatly refused to drive the Mercedes or the slightly smaller BMW in the garage. Aunt Beatrix, mindful of her dignity, wasn't too pleased, but since Prudence assured her that it was the Fiat or nothing she allowed herself to be settled in the back of the car. Prudence, as pretty as a picture in a flowered skirt and deceptively simple blouse, drove off.

Haso's home looked even more beautiful as she drove up the drive for her second visit. 'Far too big,' observed her godmother. 'It should be full of children.'

'Well, I suppose it will be in due course once his Christabel gets started on a family.'

'Don't be vulgar, dear. Anyone would think you didn't like her.'

'I don't know her and I don't suppose I ever shall.' Prudence drew up before the door and Wigge had it open before she could get Aunt Beatrix out of the car. 'Shall I leave the car here?' she wanted to know.

Mrs Wesley addressed Wigge. 'He says yes, dear; we shall be gone before Haso gets back.'

A piece of news which for some reason she found disappointing. Perhaps she enjoyed crossing swords with him? She wasn't sure.

They had coffee on the wide veranda behind the house, overlooking wide lawns and lavish flowerbeds, and Prudence found Mevrouw ter Brons Huizinga even nicer

than last time. She had a way with Aunt Beatrix too;
her quiet voice, in contrast to Beatrix's ringing tones,
soothing that lady's disgruntled comments about her
diabetes. Lunch, when they sat down to it, was composed largely of dishes which Mrs Wesley was able to
enjoy. As for Prudence, she barely noticed what she ate;
her surroundings had caught her attention, and while
she made polite conversation she contrived to look
around her. The room was beautiful, with a plaster
ceiling, its central oval panel moulded into motifs of fruit
and flowers, its plain white walls hung with paintings.
The chimneypiece was of a rococo design with candle
holders, gilded woodwork and a vast mirrored wall, and
the table they sat at was of walnut with a marquetry
border and capable of accommodating a dozen people.
She was hazy about dates, but she was almost sure that
the chairs were ribband-backed. She longed to know,
but it would hardly do to ask.

They had their coffee at the table when Mevrouw ter
Brons Huizinga said kindly, 'Do go into the gardens,
Prudence. You must be longing to—there is plenty to
see.' She looked wistful, and Prudence wondered if she
would have like to have gone with her instead of staying
in the drawing-room listening to Aunt Beatrix, who, kind
though she was, was a remorseless talker.

The afternoon was splendid. Prudence roamed right
round the outside of the house, stopping every few yards
to admire it. I could live here, she reflected, staring up
at the large windows with their gleaming paintwork, and
round the back, where the windows were quite different,
smaller and narrow and latticed. The brickwork was

older too, the house must have been added to from time to time.

She came back to where she had started and took a wide path under a pergola which would be a picture in a week or two. The path was brick, bordered by lavender hedges not yet in flower, and led eventually to a small pavilion with a pointed roof and a stone seat running all round it. The door opened when she tried it, to discover that it was furnished in a simple fashion with a chair or two and a small table. It was chilly there; she went out again, shutting the door behind her, and took a small path to one side, turning and twisting between thick shrubs and trees and which ended unexpectedly at a swimming pool, nicely screened by trees and with a small dressing-room on its further side. She sat down on a rustic wooden seat close to the pool, and it took some time to take it all in.

'Paradise,' she said out loud. 'Well, not quite—there ought to be two people in love. Paradise for two,' she sighed, 'that sounds like a popular song! I'll have to make do with just me.'

But there was no need for that; she got to her feet as she heard voices, although she wasn't sure from which direction they came. It was several seconds before Haso and his companion appeared on the other side of the pool. He stopped when he saw her and called across it. 'Oh, hello. All on your own?'

That's a silly remark, thought Prudence crossly, smiling brilliantly at the same time. The smile was for his benefit but, more than that, for the girl with him. Exactly as I'd thought, decided Prudence with satisfaction, taking a good look: a tall girl, so slim that she was thin, her dress hanging from her shoulders with no curves to fill it out. Her hair was fair, cut in a straight fringe and hanging almost to her shoulders, and her features were regular in a pale face. Her eyes would be blue, decided Prudence, although she was too far away to be sure of that, but she wasn't so far that she could see the instant antipathy towards herself. Probably Haso had told her all about the uneasy relationship between herself and him.

Haso was strolling round the pool to join her and the girl was coming with him. 'Why did you drive Wim's car?' he asked idly.

'Because I'm too scared to drive your Aunt's Mercedes,' said Prudence coolly, and looked pointedly at the girl.

'This is Christabel van Bijl—Christabel, this is Prudence Makepeace.'

'Ah, the English nurse,' Christabel smiled, her eyes like blue flints. 'Haso has told me all about you.' She offered a limp hand and Prudence gave it a good hearty shake, and she made a show of rubbing it gently. 'How strong you are—I'm sure my hand will be bruised! However, I dare say you need to be sturdy in your particular job.'

'Well, yes, but that's a good thing, isn't it? We can look after the weaklings.'

Haso said something which sounded like 'Fifteen all' and went on smoothly, 'Shall we go back to the house for tea?' And he led the way back along the narrow path with Prudence behind him and Christabel at the back.

'You have explored the gardens?' he wanted to know.

'Not quite. What I've seen is charming. The back of the house is older than the rest of it, isn't it?'

'Seventeenth-century—the front is a hundred and fifty years later...'

They had reached the house and went in through the side door, across the hall and into the drawing-room, to find his mother and aunt sitting by the windows opening on to the veranda, the tea-table between them.

Christabel gushed over the two elderly ladies with a charm which made Prudence grit her splendid teeth. The girl finally sat down between them, declaring that a cup of tea was just what she wanted most—no sugar or milk—so fattening, she said with a sly glance at Prudence. 'And I'd adore one of those little cakes, but I simply don't dare.' She picked up the plate of sugary tarts and handed them to Aunt Beatrix, who foolishly took one.

Prudence darted out of her chair and whisked it away just as her aunt was about to take a bite. She said in a calm, reproving voice, 'That was a near thing. So sorry to jump on you like that, Aunt, but I dare say Christabel didn't know about your diet.'

There was a plate of bread and butter on the table— very unusual in a Dutch house, but put there specially for Mrs Wesley. Cordelia offered it now, saying in her quiet voice, 'How very fortunate that Prudence was so quick. It must be so tiresome to get used to these changes all at once, but I'm sure you will find it less irksome in time.'

She smiled around, pouring oil on troubled waters, for Mrs Wesley was poking peevishly at her bread and butter and Christabel was uttering an angry laugh. 'My nerves really won't stand it,' she complained prettily, 'and how was I to know?' She raised blue eyes to Haso, standing a little to one side, and gave him a quivering smile.

He said blandly, 'I told you, but there is no need to fuss, there is no harm done.'

He strolled over to Prudence and sat down beside her. 'Very efficient,' he observed softly, 'and despite your size, very swift on the feet.'

'You were nearer,' she told him.

'I was so sure you would deal with the situation, and after all, I've already done a hard day's work.'

Prudence bit into a cucumber sandwich.

'Have you really? A short day, surely—you were home at half-past three.'

'Ah, yes, but I began at five o'clock this morning.'

She refused to feel sympathy. 'Doctors must expect to work irregular hours.'

'I thought you would say that . . .' He was interrupted by Christabel, who called across the room to ask what they were talking about, but she didn't wait for a reply but added with a light laugh, 'Boring old hospital talk, I suppose. What a good thing that you have me to see you have some sort of social life!'

Haso had got up to hand round second cups of tea and didn't reply. There was nothing in his face to show any annoyance, but Prudence thought that under all that massive calm he was seething.

'We're going to the theatre in Leeuwarden this evening,' remarked Christabel chattily, 'a rather special ballet. Do you enjoy ballet, Prudence?'

'Yes, very much . . .'

She wasn't given the chance to say any more, for Christabel went on, 'When I was younger I took ballet lessons—I was considered quite good, but I grew too tall.'

'One needs plenty of stamina,' observed Prudence sweetly.

Aunt Beatrix got up to go home presently, and everyone went on to the steps to see them drive away. 'You must come again,' said Mevrouw ter Brons Huizinga. 'On your own—I'm longing to take you round the garden myself.'

She leaned forward and kissed Prudence's cheek and stood waving as they drove away. 'Such a nice girl,' she observed as they went back into the house, 'and so sensible, too.'

Christabel gave a tinkling laugh. 'And so very big!' She turned to Haso. 'Drive me back now, will you, Haso, and come and fetch me at eight o'clock?'

'I'll drive you back, but I have to go to the hospital again—I shan't be free this evening. I did warn you that I can never be sure of my evenings—or my days, for that matter.'

'It's too bad! It's ridiculous that you can't take time off when you want.'

A silly remark that he didn't think was worth answering. He waited patiently while she bade his mother goodbye, kissed his parent and drove Christabel away.

Mevrouw ter Brons Huizinga went and sat down again and picked up her knitting, and Wigge came in to close the veranda doors and clear the tea-things.

'That's a nice young lady, mevrouw,' he observed with the dignified familiarity of an old family servant. He spoke in Fries and she replied in the same tongue.

'Yes, Wigge, and very pretty too.'

'That she is, and a good head on her shoulders, as they say.'

He went away at a stately pace, and Mevrouw ter Brons Huizinga laid her knitting aside. 'Such a pity,' she addressed the empty room. 'They're made for each other and neither of them knows it. And one dare not interfere.'

She went to the telephone and sat down beside it and had a lengthy talk with each of her three daughters.

Back at Aunt Emma's house her sister gave her a résumé of the day.

'Delightful. Cordelia is such a sweet person, and lunch was delicious—I was able to eat almost everything on the table, so very thoughtful of her! That Christabel girl came in at tea time with Haso—far too thin and quite shrewish. I do hope dear Haso doesn't allow himself to get caught—she's very possessive, I noticed.'

'Haso, to the best of my knowledge, has never done anything he hasn't wanted to do. Did Prudence enjoy herself?'

'I believe so—she went into the gardens after lunch and returned with Haso and that girl. They must have met somewhere there. I don't think the two girls liked each other.'

'Probably not. What is more to the point, is Haso interested in Prudence?'

Aunt Beatrix shook her head regretfully. 'If he is, he's concealing it most admirably.'

But Prudence was interested in Haso, not perhaps in the way her aunts would wish. She was sorry for him; she thought Christabel a dreadful girl, quite unsuitable to be his wife. She didn't know exactly what his status was, but she presumed he was a partner in a firm of doctors in Leeuwarden, and if he wanted to make his way in the medical world, then Christabel was going to be of no use to him, bleating on about the ballet and expecting him to be at her beck and call. Of course, she reminded herself, he deserved every inch of the girl, not that that would amount to much, she resembled nothing so much as a telegraph pole...

It was a waste of time thinking about the wretched man. She showered and changed and went down to join the aunts for the evening.

Two days later Mevrouw ter Brons Huizinga telephoned and invited her to spend the day. 'Just me,' she was told, 'and perhaps my youngest daughter—she has been on her own for a short time and Haso let her have Prince, his dog, to keep her company, but her husband is home again and she will be bringing him back. You can drive yourself over? Haso is in Leiden for a few days.'

When, wondered Prudence thoughtfully, did that man ever do any work? 'I'd love to come,' she said warmly. 'I must just see to the aunts after breakfast, but that won't take long as they are expecting old friends for lunch.'

She went to tell the aunts, and then to Wim to see if he would let her have his car again. She had picked up a few words of Dutch by now. 'Tomorrow morning?' she asked, and added in English, 'I'll be very careful.'

Wim smiled benevolently and said, *'Ja, ja'* several times, waving his arms to make sure that she understood, and she skipped up to her room, intent on deciding what she would wear. The weather was turning warmer, although there was always a cool breeze; she settled on a cotton top and matching cardigan and her flowered skirt. A pity Haso wouldn't be there...

The aunts were unexpectedly undemanding in the morning, and it was half-past ten as Prudence got into Wim's car and drove carefully out of the gates. The day was as fine as she had hoped it would be, and the country around her was green and lush under the wide blue sky. She didn't hurry, anticipating the delight she would feel when she reached the drive to the house and would get her first glimpse of it.

It was even better than she remembered. She slowed the car so that she could study it at leisure and presently stopped outside its door, where Wigge was already waiting.

There was another car parked on the sweep—a racy sports model. Just for a moment Prudence wondered if Haso had returned, and then she remembered that his sister would have driven over from Groningen.

Mother and daughter were sitting on the veranda, a tray of coffee on the table. With them was a large, fierce-looking dog with a shaggy black coat and yellow eyes. As Prudence joined them, Mevrouw ter Brons Huizinga spoke quietly to him and he got up and pranced to meet her. Prudence offered a balled fist, then rubbed the great woolly head, and her hostess said, 'Oh, good—you like each other. He's Haso's dog, but he's been taught to be civil to our friends. This is Sebeltsje, my youngest daughter.'

The girls shook hands, liking each other at once. Sebeltsje was almost as tall as Prudence, with pale hair and blue eyes and a pretty face, and nicely plump too. 'I knew Prince would like you,' she exclaimed. 'He looks fierce, doesn't he? And he can be, too. You like dogs?'

Prudence sat down and accepted the coffee offered to her. 'Yes, very much—I don't think we've got his kind at home, though. He's a bouvier, isn't he?'

'Aert—my husband—has promised me a puppy for my birthday.'

They talked idly for an hour before lunch, and after that meal Prudence was borne off by the pair of them, with Prince tramping at their heels, to enjoy a protracted tour of the gardens. It took quite a time and Mevrouw ter Brons Huizinga suggested that they went to the drawing-room and had tea. 'Sebeltsje will have to go soon, as Aert will be home.'

'He's a doctor,' explained Sebeltsje. 'Not in the same street as Haso, of course, but he is much younger. Besides, I tell him that one learned professor in the family is quite enough.'

'A professor?' Prudence did her best to sound casual.

'Oh, yes. He's senior partner in a practice too, but he does a lot of consulting work as well...' She broke off and got up to look out of the window. 'And there he is—look at Prince!'

The dog had gone to the door, his nose pressed against it, his stump of a tail wagging furiously, rumbling happily to himself. Sebeltsje opened the door and he pranced through and could be heard barking happily in the hall.

Haso was talking to him, and Prudence was glad she
had a few moments in which to regain the calm she had
lost at the sound of his arrival. A calm she immediately
lost again as he came into the room, kissed his mother
and sister, looked at her with raised eyebrows and then
walked across to where she was sitting and kissed her
too.

'An unexpected pleasure,' he said smoothly, so that
she didn't know if he was pleased or annoyed to find
her there. She ignored the kiss—she could think about
that later—and gave him a genial smile.

'Glad to see me?' he wanted to know, and accepted
tea from his mother and came to sit next her.

'Well, I . . . that is, I thought you were away from
home.'

'And now I'm here. If you have any questions about
the aunts I shall be happy to answer them.'

Prudence was saved from answering him by his sister,
who got to her feet, declaring that she would have to
go. 'You must come and see me, Prudence,' she said.
'Could you drive over? Or better still, Haso could give
you a lift next time he comes to Groningen.'

'I could drive,' said Prudence, so quickly that Haso
gave a crack of laughter, and to her great annoyance she
blushed.

She left soon after that, seen off by her hostess and
Haso, who evinced no wish to see her again, and certainly a trip to Groningen wasn't mentioned. Which,
considering her forceful reply that she would drive
herself, was hardly surprising.

CHAPTER FOUR

Two days later Prudence was sitting in the drawing-room with her aunts, who were entertaining two friends to coffee—an old lady, tall and thin and beaky-nosed, who, she felt sure, disapproved of her on sight, and a slightly younger lady, very self-effacing and speaking only when spoken to. The conversation was terribly stilted and carried on mostly by the old lady in Dutch, although from time to time she addressed herself to Prudence, but as her remarks were for the most part searching questions about her work, home life and family, which Prudence answered politely but briefly, she gave up and began a lengthy conversation with Aunt Emma and Aunt Beatrix, which left Prudence stranded with the self-effacing lady, who spoke rather less English than Prudence did Dutch.

Which perhaps accounted for the look of pleasure on her face when Haso walked into the room. He greeted his aunts, shook the old lady's hand and that of her companion and nodded to Prudence. The old lady smiled graciously at him and the younger one simpered. Prudence gave him a wooden look and said nothing.

He didn't sit down, but stood with a hand of the back of Aunt Emma's chair, listening to the old lady holding forth. Prudence, not understanding a word, did her best to look interested, aware that her face bore all the animation of a cod's on a fishmonger's slab. Suddenly she wanted to be at home with Aunt Maud, going to the village shop, exchanging good-days with people she had known for years; their soft country voices music to her ears after the old lady's strident, high-pitched voice.

The doctor, watching her under his lids, smiled to himself, brought the conversation to a gentle close and said, 'I'm on my way to Groningen. I wondered if you would like to see Sebeltsje, Prudence? She phoned just now and invited you to lunch.' He turned to look at his aunts. 'No one has any plans?'

The aunts were instantly enthusiastic. 'How delightful! Prudence, you will like to see Groningen, won't you? I'm sure Haso will willingly wait a few minutes while you tidy yourself.'

They were all looking at her, the ladies with satisfaction because she was to have an unexpected treat, and the doctor with no expression on his face at all.

'I'm not sure...' she began, to be interrupted by his bland,

'Sebeltsje told me she wouldn't speak to me again if I didn't bring you.'

She got to her feet. 'I'll get my handbag.'

She contrived to do her face, run a comb through her hair and spray on a dash of Lumière before she went back to the drawing-room, where she wished her aunts goodbye, then shook hands with the disapproving old lady and her timid companion before being ushered out of the house and into the Daimler.

Prince was sitting in the back; he grinned at her as she got into the car and they drove off, and he pushed his great head between them, breathing hotly down her neck and rolling his eyes with pleasure.

'Does he go everywhere with you?' she asked. There was something about the doctor's silence which made her anxious to break it.

'Almost always.'

'You've had him for a long time?'

'Two years. I found him tied to a lamppost in several inches of snow. He must have been all of four months old.'

Prudence put up a hand to stroke the shaggy head. 'Oh, the poor scrap! He's quite beautiful, too...'

'A fierce fighter and a splendid bodyguard. When I'm away and have to leave him at home, he guards my mother so closely, she can go nowhere without him.'

He drove for a little while in silence again and she looked out the window, trying to think of a topic of conversation. They were on a quiet country road, and when they reached a crossroads and went across instead of turning on to what was obviously the main road, she asked, 'Is this another way to Groningen?'

'Indeed it is, and much more interesting than the main road.'

As indeed it was, with a canal running beside it until they had almost reached the city, when he turned off on to the motorway which led to its heart.

Prudence looked around her with interest. Groningen was a good deal larger than Leeuwarden, with some splendid houses and numerous canals. The doctor threaded his way through the busy streets and presently turned into a narrow street, drove over a high-backed bridge above a canal and turned carefully into a cobbled square. Halfway along one side he stopped.

'Sebeltsje's husband is a doctor at the University—
it's close by, although you can't see the building from
here.' He got out and opened her door, and then let
Prince out too.

The house was rather tall and narrow, with a mirror-
back gable and leaded windows and worn stone steps
leading up to its door. Haso pulled the old-fashioned
bell and his sister came to the door. She flung her arms
around him and smiled widely at Prudence. 'Oh, good—
I did so hope you'd come. Haso, can you stay for lunch?'

She tweaked Prince's ears and he leant lovingly against
her.

'No, sorry. Shall I leave Prince with you?' Haso spoke
to Prudence. 'I'll collect you about five o'clock.'

He said a casual goodbye and took himself off, and
Sebeltsje took Prudence's arm. 'Come into the sitting-
room, we'll have coffee.' She led the way into a high-
ceilinged room overlooking the street, furnished
comfortably. It had panelled walls and there was a door
in the wall facing the window. A stout woman came
through it as they sat down.

'This is Joke—she looks after us.' Prudence smiled at
her, and the woman smiled back and spoke to Sebeltsje
and went away again, while Prince sat down between
them, his eyes on two kittens curled up on one of the
chairs. His yellow stare must have roused them, for they
woke up, stretched, gave him a cursory glance and went
back to sleep again.

'He's very fond of them,' explained Sebeltsje. 'Most
bouviers are pretty fierce, but he's sweet with anything
which belongs to the family, and of course he adores
Haso.'

It was obvious that his sister adored her brother, too. She had a great deal to say about him as they drank their coffee. 'And now this awful van Bijl girl's after him. None of us can stand her, although she's very suitable for a wife. I suppose that's why he'll probably marry her. He's not in love with her—I asked him, and he said that since he hadn't fallen in love with any girl enough to want to marry her he'd settle for someone who would fit in with his life. Only, of course, she's trying to alter that; always fussing him to go here and there and all over the place with her.'

Prudence listened to these artless remarks with a good deal of interest. It was a pity that since Haso didn't love anyone he should have picked on Christabel for his future wife; couldn't he see that within a few years they would either not be on speaking terms or he would have given in to her wishes for a social life? For a clever man, high in his profession, he was singularly stupid. But then, clever men seldom had much interest in anything but what they happened to be clever at.

She didn't voice her thoughts, but murmured in an understanding way and fed Prince a biscuit which he swallowed at one gulp, his eyes blissfully closed.

'You are bored at the aunts' house?' Sebeltsje's question took Prudence by surprise.

'Well, no—it's a lovely lazy life and I have to keep an eye on them both. Besides, it's foreign.'

'Have you got a boyfriend?'

'No—no one in particular. But that's not quite true. There's Walter—I've known him for years and he rather took it for granted that I'd marry him...'

'So why don't you?'

'I don't love him.'

'Oh, well, of course you can't, can you? I was almost
engaged to someone when I met Aert, and I knew at
once that I wanted to marry Aert.' Sebeltsje added with
certainty, 'You always know.' She got up and poured
sherry into two glasses. 'Mama told me that the aunts
were planning a holiday in Guernsey. You'll go with
them?'

'They've asked me if I would go with them, and I
suppose I shall. Though I ought to be looking out for
a job...'

'Why don't you get one here, in Holland? There are
several English nurses in the hospital here and
in Leeuwarden—they get Dutch lessons to start with,
but many of the medical terms are the same in both
languages. Haso would find you a job—he's on the hospital committee and people listen to him.'

Just for a moment Prudence toyed with the idea—
what a chance to prove to him that she was a good nurse!
She said mendaciously, 'I've already applied for a job
in Scotland—the vacancy isn't until August and I told
them I would go for an interview when I got back.'

'Scotland? We spent our honeymoon there—I liked
it. Perhaps you'll marry a Scotsman.'

'But you were married here?' A question which led
naturally enough to a detailed account of the wedding,
which lasted until they had had their lunch. They didn't
hurry over the meal; they liked each other and there was
plenty to talk about. By the time Prudence had been
shown round the house and the long, narrow garden
behind it, the afternoon was well advanced, and Aert
arrived home just as Joke brought in the tea-tray. He

was tall and thick-set, fair-haired and blue-eyed and nice-looking in a blunt-featured fashion. He kissed his wife, shook hands with Prudence and observed, 'Haso's coming for tea; the last two cases on his list weren't fit enough for surgery.'

'Oh, is he a surgeon?' asked Prudence.

They both looked at her in surprise. 'Didn't you know? Of course, he wouldn't tell you himself—he's a professor of surgery and operates here and in Leeuwarden, besides being a consultant at Leeuwarden and Amsterdam. Does quite a bit of travelling too, here, there and everywhere.'

Prudence felt her face flame. 'I thought he was a GP.'

She went even pinker when she looked up and saw Haso standing in the open doorway. He gave her a mocking smile as he crossed the room and sat down, but although he must have heard her he made no comment, only accepted a cup of tea with a casual greeting to his sister and Aert and immediately started on a gentle conversation about nothing much which lasted until he observed, 'I hate to break up this pleasant half-hour, but I've got a date this evening and I must deliver Prudence back safely.'

She bade her adieux unfussily, thanked Sebeltsje and was ushered into the Daimler, where she sat quietly while Prince, delighted to be with his master again, scrambled into the back of the car and, when Haso got in, rested his great head on her shoulder.

'Push him off if you don't want him panting down your neck,' said Haso.

'I don't mind.' Seeking a safe topic of conversation, she said, 'Have you had a busy day?'

'Yes. I shall be in tomorrow morning to give Aunt Emma a thorough overhaul. If she's fit, there's no reason why she and Aunt Beatrix shouldn't go on holiday whenever they want to. Aunt Beatrix seems stabilised.'

There had been no warmth in his voice; he might have been giving directions to a ward Sister. Prudence swallowed the words she longed to utter. 'Very well, Doctor,' matched his cool tones.

She sat silent, reflecting that he was the most dis-agreeable man she had ever met. She disliked Christabel too, but she found it in her heart to be sorry for the girl. Upon reflection, she felt sorry for Haso too.

Rather to her surprise, he went indoors with her when they arrived at Emma's house. The two ladies were seated one each side of a small rent table, each knitting some intricately patterned garment.

'There you are, my dears,' observed Aunt Emma. 'I'm sure you have had a delightful day together. Haso, touch the bell if you will—you will join us in a glass of sherry?'

'Regretfully, no. I'm already a little late, but I shall be here tomorrow morning to make sure that you're both fit to go on holiday.'

He kissed them in turn and went to the door. 'Prudence, I thought we might have dinner together tomorrow. I'll come for you around seven o'clock.'

The last thing she had expected to hear; her pretty mouth hung open in surprise, and by the time she had shut it, preparatory to making a cool refusal, he had gone.

'How delightful!' declared Aunt Beatrix. 'Haso can be such an amusing companion. So kind of him to take you out—you will enjoy every minute of it.'

Prudence said nothing, already planning a really awful headache which would start round about six o'clock in the evening of the next day and get worse.

When the telephone rang the next morning she went to answer it since there was no one else around. 'I should have warned you,' said Haso's voice in her ear. 'It won't be in the least use having a headache, I shall come and haul you out of bed and take you to dine in your nightie. A charming one, if I remember aright.'

Prudence took a swelling breath. 'Well, of all the nerve! I won't...'

She need not have bothered to speak. 'Wear a pretty dress.' He had hung up before she could say a word more.

She spent the day telling herself she wasn't going out with him, but somehow she found herself getting into the dark blue dress after spending a good deal longer than usual over her face and hair. Going reluctantly downstairs a few minutes after half-past seven, she found Haso sitting with his aunts, listening gravely to them. A purely social visit; he had been as he had promised that morning, but his manner then, that of a consultant visiting his ward, had hardly been conducive to personal remarks of any kind—indeed, beyond a few questions and directions as to his relations' treatment, he had had nothing to say.

He got to his feet as she went into the room, and greeted her just as though they hadn't seen each other already that day. 'If there's one thing which teaches a girl to be punctual,' he observed bluntly, 'it's a nurse's training.'

A remark which Prudence found extremely vexing. All the same, she wasn't going to let him have the satis-

faction of needling her. She smiled distantly at him, bade
her aunts goodbye and accompanied him out to the car,
glad she had taken so much trouble with her appearance, matching his elegance.

She wasn't going to ask where they were going; she
had been dragooned into the evening, and good manners,
she hoped, would see that she behaved politely towards
him, but she wasn't going to show any interest. She
would, she resolved silently, be the dullest companion
he had ever had the misfortune to entertain.

All the same, she was surprised when he took a small
side road once they had left the village, instead of the
main road which would have taken them either to
Leeuwarden or Groningen. With a tremendous effort she
refrained from asking where they were going. Instead
she remarked upon the pleasant evening, the charm of
the landscape and a variety of remarks about the forth-
coming holiday in Guernsey, to all of which Haso replied in monosyllables, so that presently she gave up.

After another mile or so of silence she remarked tartly,
'I can't think why you've asked me out, because we have
no pleasure in each other's company, have we?'

'For that very reason—perhaps if we get to know each
other we might enjoy each other's company more.'

'Yes, that's all very well, but I'm leaving shortly.'

'So you are at pains to remind me. Do you want to
know where we're going?'

'Yes.'

'Roodkerk—quite close by but difficult to reach, it's
off the main road. There's a restaurant there—De
Trochreed. Perhaps you don't know that in Europe
there's a chain of hotels and restaurants under the name

Romantic—I must add that the title implies atmosphere, good service and food and private ownership—one does not have to be romantically inclined to patronise them.'

He slowed the car. 'Here we are.'

Probably Haso was right and one didn't need to feel romantically inclined to dine there, but certainly the restaurant was conducive to romance with its soft lighting, candlelit tables, beautifully appointed, and the welcome as they went in.

The doctor was known; they were ushered to the small bar where they had their drinks and chose their meal before going to their table. The place was nearly full and Prudence, glancing around her, was glad she was wearing the blue dress, for the women there were very well turned out.

She had allowed Haso to advise her as to what she should eat, and since the menu was wildly expensive she made no demur. New herrings, served in slivers on toast, because that was a favourite of the Dutch during the early summer; lobster served with a mouthwatering salad and tiny new potatoes, and an elaborate ice-cream dish smothered in whipped cream. She had a splendid appetite, and, although she hadn't wanted to come in the first place, the good food and her companion's casual talk were turning the evening into an unexpectedly enjoyable outing. By the time she was embarking on the ice-cream she had quite forgotten that she didn't like him, and was laughing and talking as though they were the best of friends.

It was as they were drinking their coffee that she said suddenly, 'Do you bring Christabel here?'

'Oh, yes, on numerous occasions.' His smile mocked her. 'She likes only the best restaurants. Women like to dress up and go to elegant places, don't they?'

She gave him a fiercely defiant look. 'Actually, I like fish and chips wrapped in a newspaper parcel and those coffee stalls where you can buy a mug of tea so strong that a mouse can trot on it, and cheese and pickle sandwiches.' Haso was staring at her with raised eyebrows and she hurried to add, 'I don't mean to be rude; this is super and I love dressing up...' She frowned a little, intent on explaining. 'What I mean is, it's the company which is important, isn't it?' She caught his eye and went pink. 'I haven't... I've made a mess of it.'

He said silkily, 'On the contrary, you have made yourself very clear. I can only hope that dinner compensates for my company!'

Prudence felt her cheeks burn. 'I'm so sorry—that isn't what I meant at all. At least... that is, I didn't want you to think I was the kind of girl who took umbrage if she didn't get the best of everything.'

'And what kind of a girl do you suppose I think you are?' He was leaning back in his chair, looking amused, which annoyed her, but she owed him an apology.

'Well, you don't like me—you never have, but that's my fault; I was annoyed because the first time we met you pretended to be the gardener.'

'My dear girl, I did nothing of the sort. It was hardly my fault if you chose to draw erroneous conclusions.'

It became suddenly important that he should tell her whether he liked her or not. 'Why don't you like me?' she repeated.

'And if I ask you the same question, do I get a truthful answer? I think not. I suspect that neither of us is quite ready to answer that.'

He smiled at her, and this time it wasn't even faintly mocking, but gentle and kind, so that she smiled back. After a moment she said, 'I expect you're right. It's called agreeing to differ.' In case he didn't quite understand, she explained, 'It means that we don't see eye to eye, but respect one another's opinions.'

'Armed neutrality—it sounds a splendid solution.' He lifted a finger to a hovering waiter. 'Let's drink to it.'

Champagne—on top of the sherry and the two glasses of hock. Prudence sipped cautiously. She had been brought up never to mix her drinks, and she wondered if she should refuse. But that wouldn't do at all; Haso had offered an olive branch of sorts, and she must accept it gratefully. She enjoyed the first glass so much that she accepted another.

'May you drink and drive in Holland?' she wanted to know.

'Certainly not. We'll have some more coffee presently if you're nervous at the idea of me driving while under the influence.'

He appeared as calm and casual as usual. She said, 'I'm not nervous; I don't suppose you would be so foolish.'

The restaurant was half-empty now and Prudence glanced at her watch. She gave the doctor an astonished look. 'Do you know what the time is? It's after eleven o'clock!'

He raised his eyebrows. 'My dear Prudence, you sound like the kitchenmaid on her evening out!'

She forgot about the armed neutrality. 'Well, of all the nasty things to say! You're the rudest man... I'm so sorry for your Christabel.'

She hadn't meant to say that, but the champagne, backed up by sherry and hock, had the hold of her tongue.

He smiled, not the gentle smile which had so delighted her, but a nasty curl of the lip. 'Shall we leave Christabel out of it?'

Prudence went red and took a last drink of champagne. 'I'm sorry. But your remark was beastly and I forgot that we'd agreed to differ. I've enjoyed my evening very much, thank you, and dinner was heavenly, only now I think I'd better go home.' She added, 'Before we quarrel.'

He laughed. 'Living up to your most unsuitable name?' He signalled for the bill and she said thoughtfully, 'Well, at least we've tried—to be friends, I mean.'

'Indeed, yes. But I feel that we should persevere— what is it you say? "If at first you don't succeed, try, try try again"? A remarkably sensible injunction. We might even manage to say goodbye with some semblance of regret.'

For some reason the idea didn't appeal to her. Haso annoyed her excessively, but all the same she was going to miss him. She sighed at the thought, and he watched her with a gleam in his eyes and a glimmer of a smile.

He drove back unhurriedly through the clear night, carrying on a mild conversation about nothing much which required only the minimum of answers and certainly didn't provoke her once. He got out at his aunt's house and saw her inside, at the same time wishing her goodnight in a manner which reminded her strongly of an elder brother or even a kindly uncle.

Undressing slowly, Prudence reflected that if this was armed neutrality it was going to be very dull.

She made suitable replies to her aunt's questions, rather coyly put, the following morning. Yes, she had had a delightful time, dinner had been delicious, the restaurant quite charming...

'Dear Haso is such a pleasant companion?' suggested Aunt Beatrix.

Prudence said cautiously that they had had a lot to talk about.

'Naturally. I expect he'll take you out again before we go to Guernsey.'

'What about Christabel?'

'She's in Italy, dear, visiting art galleries. She thinks that culture is very important, especially for a person of her kind...'

'What kind is she?' asked Prudence, allowing curiosity to take over.

'*Adel,* dear. Her position in life is very important to her. If—and I say if—she manages to get herself married to Haso, which I for one very much doubt, she will do her best to make him take his proper place in society.'

'But he's got a place—he's a medical man, and from what I can discover very well thought of.'

'He is also from *adel*, but we as a family have never considered that important.' It was Aunt Emma who spoke. 'Haso is the head of the family now, but he doesn't use his title, and although we have friends all over Holland, we make no push to go into social circles.'

'Well, well,' observed Prudence, 'I do live and learn, don't I?'

Haso came two days later, kissed his aunts, nodded coolly to Prudence and observed, 'Well, everything is arranged, Aunt Emma. You have a late morning flight from Schiphol the day after tomorrow. Wim can drive you down. You'll be met at the airport and taken to your hotel. I've booked rooms for two weeks as you asked. I've arranged with the hotel to see to your return flight. I dare say Prudence can deal with that for you.'

He looked at her. 'I presume you will be coming back here? I don't think the aunts should travel on their own.'

'Pretty will be with them, and Aunt Emma's maid as well. I intend to fly back to England—I have to take a job, you know.'

'I can't see that a few days more will make much difference to that. You can fly back a couple of days later. You are, after all, in charge of them.'

Prudence had a scathing answer to that, only it wasn't uttered. She caught sight of the two elderly ladies watching her with scarcely concealed anxiety; to refuse to escort them back home would be more than unkind. She said with a serenity she didn't feel, 'Very well, I'll come back here, but I should be glad if arrangements could be made so that I could leave for England on the following day.'

He had got his own way, he could afford to be magnanimous. 'Give me a day or so's warning and I'll arrange that for you.' He got up to go. 'Give me a ring if you have any problems. My best wishes for a pleasant holiday. I've written to a colleague of mine at the hospital, his phone number is with the tickets.'

He had gone; the aunts fell to discussing what they should take with them and Prudence sat on a window-seat, telling herself she was glad she wouldn't see him for at least two weeks, and then only briefly, before she went back home. It was a surprisingly lowering thought.

It was almost impossible to have any thoughts of her own for the next twenty-four hours. Pretty and Sieke were pleased enough to be going on holiday, but until they arrived at the hotel they had plenty to worry them. The aunts were by no means relaxed travellers, although they had journeyed widely. They changed their minds a dozen times as to what they should take with them, in-sisted on Prudence phoning to make sure that Haso's meticulously arranged journey was indeed without any chance of hold-ups, and drove the kitchen staff off their heads with instructions as to what should be done during their absence.

It was with relief that Prudence stowed her two elderly companions into the back of the Mercedes and then got in beside them. Pretty sat with Wim, but Sieke, being on the small side, was squashed in the back. Aunt Emma complained bitterly about the lack of space, but even she had to admit that Wim wouldn't be able to drive two cars back to Friesland. Both ladies were a little out of temper by the time they arrived at Schiphol, but since Sieke and Pretty were there to deal with the luggage and Prudence shepherded them to a quiet corner where they could drink their coffee in peace, by the time their plane was called they had recovered their good humour.

The flight was accomplished in comfort; there was no lack of attention on the part of the stewardess, who plied them with drinks, magazines and offers of cushions.

When they arrived there were two cars waiting for them, the second for Pretty and Sieke and the luggage, so that the aunts could be driven in comfort the few miles to St Peter Port and the hotel.

The sun had come out after a rather gloomy morning and the road, winding between villages, was fairly empty of traffic. The hotel, when they reached it presently, looked pleasant, a Georgian mansion halfway up the outer slopes of the town, facing the harbour below and the open sea with Herm island in front and a few miles away Sark behind it. You could see Jersey on a fine day, volunteered the driver.

Haso had done his work well; they were received warmly, ushered to chairs while Prudence dealt with the desk work and then led up the wide staircase to their rooms. Haso again, thought Prudence, following behind with Sieke and Pretty, burdened with wraps and travel bags, hard on her heels, for the rooms were splendid, facing the sea, most tastefully furnished and, as far as she could see, having every comfort. Her own room, close by, although smaller, was just as comfortable. Pretty and Sieke were led away to the room they were to share on the floor above, and Prudence thoughtfully ordered a tray of tea before the aunts thought of it first.

Much refreshed, the aunts made themselves comfortable with books while Prudence made the telephone call to Haso which he had asked her to do in a manner decisive enough for her to waste no time about doing so.

His voice in her ear gave her the impression that he wasn't pleased to hear hers. She said without preamble, 'We're in the hotel and very comfortable. We had a good flight and your aunts are delighted with everything.'

She was surprised when he asked, 'And you, Prudence—are you delighted?'

'Me? It all seems very nice...'

'Well, of course. So it should be—I'm not there.'

She couldn't think of an answer to that and he didn't seem to expect one, for he said, 'Give my love to the aunts and look after them well. Goodbye, Prudence.'

She hung up pettishly. Of course she would look after his aunts, wasn't that why she had been inveigled into coming? She gave them his message, made sure that they were content to sit while their unpacking was done, and repaired to her own room, where she stood at the window for some minutes, staring at the splendid view and not seeing it, as it was completely obscured by Haso's image.

She bestirred herself at length. 'This won't do,' she admonished herself as she started to unpack. 'Anyone would think I miss him!'

Which, of course, she did, although she wasn't going to admit that, not even to herself.

The hotel was not quite full, it was too early in the season; they dined at a table in the big window overlooking the harbour, and here again Haso had seen to things. A tasty variety of dishes was offered Aunt Beatrix with due regard to her diabetes, and presented in such a way that she could find no fault, and Aunt Emma, who enjoyed her food, was pleased to compliment the floor manager as they left the restaurant. Prudence saw them both safely to their beds, made sure that Pretty and Sieke were comfortable in their room, found a woolly jacket and took herself off for a walk before bedtime.

A few minutes' walk downhill took her to the boulevard, and she walked briskly towards the centre of the town. Castle Cornet at the end of its pier looked interesting, but it would have to wait for another day when she had more time. Now she contented herself with walking as far as the town church with a quick glimpse of the arcades and shops in the narrow high street. Very continental, she reflected, retracing her steps, but she doubted if the aunts would want to spend any time there. In the morning she would see about hiring a car so that she could drive them around the island. That was something Haso had forgotten to do, she thought crossly, climbing into bed and falling at once into a dreamless sleep.

She was wrong. After breakfast, which she ate with Pretty and Sieke while the two elderly ladies had theirs in their rooms, she was handed a key at the reception desk and was told that the car hired in her name was parked opposite the bar entrance. The clerk pointed it out to her; a neat Renault, roomy enough to take the aunts in comfort.

She took the key and went to have a look at it. There was a map on the front seat, she opened it up and studied it; the island might be small, but it was full of roads. She sat down on the low stone wall which encircled the hotel gardens the better to study it.

The man who strolled over to her was youngish, not tall but slimly built and good-looking. That his eyes were a shade too close together was not noticeable unless one studied his face very closely.

'Just arrived?' he asked her, and added, 'Hello,' and held out his hand. 'Jerome Blake. I've been here for a few days—I've been before, as a matter of fact, so perhaps I could help you to plan your trips? It's a bit confusing at first.'

Prudence shook hands. 'How kind of you. I have two elderly aunts with me and I thought perhaps a drive of an hour or so at a time. They tire easily.'

He said easily. 'Ah—you're with the Dutch lady who came yesterday? And another lady?'

She didn't notice the searching look he gave her. 'That's right. We're here for a couple of weeks.'

'Then you can't do better than divide the map into four and explore each area in turn. There's plenty to see—potteries, a candle factory, a craft centre, the famous miniature church, and of course, the shops in St Peter Port.' He smiled widely. 'Perhaps they won't be too keen on shopping, but if you need an escort you have only to say, I'd be delighted to escort you. The shops are open in the evening.'

It was nice to have someone young to talk to, but he was going rather fast. She said coolly, 'Thank you, I'll remember that, but I don't expect to have much time to myself.' He looked so downcast that she smiled at him. 'I must go, but I expect I'll see you around.'

It was pleasant to meet someone who so obviously wanted to know her better, unlike some men she knew, reflected Prudence sourly, but she wasn't sure if she liked him. She dismissed him from her thoughts and went to see how her aunts were getting on.

That day and the next few days were spent agreeably enough. She drove her companions to various parts of the island, watched candles being made, potters at work, then visited the smallest church, and now and then en-countered Jerome Blake, who, without saying much, managed to convey his wish for her company. It was one evening, after they had dined following a pleasant afternoon's drive along the south of the island, that he came across the wide floor of the lounge where they were sitting before the aunts went to bed. He wished Prudence a good evening and addressed himself to Aunt Beatrix.

'I wonder if your niece would care to look around the shops?' he suggested with a smile. 'They're open until nine o'clock, and perhaps she has a wish to buy something.' He turned to Prudence. 'I'd be delighted to accompany you.' His smile was open and friendly and she stifled her vague feeling of dislike.

'I'd like that very much.' She turned to her aunts and found them smiling.

'Of course you should go, Prudence. Certainly we must take some trifle back with us—see what you can find. We shall sit here until ten o'clock, and if you are not back Pretty and Sieke will see us safely to our beds.'

'I'll fetch a jacket,' said Prudence. The prospect of shopping was delightful; Aunt Beatrix was well stabilised and Aunt Emma, although she couldn't do much, was almost her old self. She went in search of Pretty and told her she would be back some time after ten o'clock, and very much to her surprise she found that lady agreeable.

'For you've had no fun at all so far, Miss Prudence,' said Pretty. 'Sieke and me, we've had time enough to go into the town and enjoy ourselves while you've been driving the car here, there and everywhere. You go and enjoy yourself.'

So Prudence bade her aunts goodnight and joined Jerome Blake outside the hotel entrance, prepared to do just that.

It was unfortunate that Haso should telephone that evening. It was Pretty who took the call and, undeterred by his harsh voice demanding to know where Prudence was, gave a satisfactory report of his aunts and added, 'And Miss Prudence has gone off to spend the evening with ever such a nice man—gone to the shops, they have. The first few hours she's had to herself since we got here.' She sounded accusing. 'Driving Madam and Mevrouw around all day long and playing patience with them every evening—it's not natural!'

'Tell her I'll telephone tomorrow evening,' said the doctor, and rang off.

CHAPTER FIVE

PRUDENCE, happily unaware of Haso's phone call, spent the evening looking in shop windows. Jerome Blake was a good guide. He showed her the best shops in the high street and the arcade, pointed out the covered market where she might get the chance of visiting one morning, and took her away from the high street, up a narrow, winding street lined with boutiques, antique shops and expensive jewellers. The shops were shut, but there was plenty to see. She would, she decided silently, find time to come on her own before they went back to Holland. She hadn't much money with her, but she had her Access card, and the clothes were exactly to her taste.

They stopped for coffee on the way back, and Jerome treated her with just the right amount of casual friendliness to make her uncertain of her initial wariness of him. At the hotel he saw her into the reception lobby, wished her a cheerful goodnight and went away, with the casual hope that they might have a similar outing before she left.

Perhaps she had been too hasty in her judgement of him, she thought uncertainly as she got ready for bed.

Pretty gave her Haso's message at breakfast, but only the part of it concerning his intention of telephoning that evening. She thought it a great pity that the two of them couldn't hit it off; she was sure her madam had hoped they would have an instant liking for each other,

92

instead of which they were at daggers drawn. Pretty and Sieke, discussing it together in their mixture of English and Dutch, agreed that it was a crying shame.

Haso wasted no time in niceties when he telephoned that evening. 'You were out,' declared his voice coldly.

She snapped back at him, 'Yes, I was—for the first time since we arrived. And since you feel the need to poke your nose into my affairs, I had a pleasant evening with someone—a man—who's staying at the hotel.'

He said with infuriating calm, 'I'm not in the least interested in your life, Prudence, and I'm not at all sure why you should be so edgy. You're free to do what you like and go out with whom you please if and when my aunts are in good hands other than your own.' Which made her feel foolish. She wasn't going to say she was sorry; she gave a succinct report on both ladies and waited to hear what he had to say.

Very little and that uttered in a tone which held no apology. Prudence put down the receiver and flounced back to the aunts, waiting to play their usual nightly game of Patience.

'Was that dear Haso?' asked Aunt Emma in her rather loud, clear voice. 'How good of him to telephone!'

Prudence sat down, her colour high. 'He sends you his love,' she announced. 'He just wanted to know how you both were.'

Aunt Beatrix said in a vaguely questioning way, 'That young man—Mr Blake?—came to say if you were free would you like to go for a walk, but I told him that we had been out for a good deal of the day and you were too tired.'

Prudence put two packs of cards on the table, biting back an angry retort. The aunts were dears, but they had no business interfering with other people's lives. She had seen Jerome Blake standing by the window in the second lounge across the hall. She said quietly, 'I'm going for a walk with him—just for an hour. I'm not in the least tired, and he's a pleasant companion. I'll be back before your bedtime.'

She smiled at their surprised faces and went in search of Jerome Blake, who was to be seen still standing at the window with his back to the room, looking out to the harbour.

She said unselfconsciously, 'The aunts made a mistake—I'm not in the least tired and I'd love a short walk. Will you wait while I get a wrap?'

He was flatteringly pleased to see her; his obvious pleasure in her company was something after Haso's brisk dismissal of her. Prudence went up to her room, leaving him to mull over his edifying thoughts. A very pretty girl and no fool, but better than that, owning two aunts who, according to the receptionist's guarded answers to his carelessly put questions, were extremely well-to-do, and although she was rather vague about it, she believed one of them had a title—a Dutch title, of course. He would have to be careful with the girl, of course, she wasn't the kind to have the wool pulled over her eyes, but there was a week still. He would have to find out exactly where she lived—presumably she would return to England eventually.

They went down the hill and turned away from the town to walk along the road leading to the Aquarium. The sun had set now, but it was still light and the sea was calm. A ferry had just come in and there was a good deal of bustle in the harbour, but their road was quite quiet save for other people strolling along it. Jerome was careful to keep the talk to trivialities to start with, before cautiously slipping in a question here and there, and Prudence, still smarting under Haso's brusque tongue, answered him without much thought. He observed casually, 'You won't like London after this and wherever you are living in Holland, will you?'

And she replied carelessly, 'Oh, but I don't intend to get a job there. I've had years of it, but now I've actually left I should hate to go back permanently. Of course there's nothing for me near my home—it's a very small village in Somerset. Someone suggested that I should get a job in Holland, and I must say that where I'm staying in Friesland is delightful, only living in hospital there, or even in digs, wouldn't be the same as living in a country house with a heavenly garden.'

Jerome murmured casually and skilfully changed the conversation; he could be amusing and he was certainly good company. Back at the hotel he bade her goodnight without any mention of further walks. Lulled by his friendly casualness, Prudence had already decided that if he asked her out again she would certainly go, unaware that that was exactly what he had been hoping for.

All the same, her last thoughts before going to sleep were of Haso. They were unsettling, but she was too sleepy to go into that.

They went to Herm the next day and, the aunts being what they were, Prudence had arranged to hire a launch for their sole use. A phone call from the reception desk had ensured that they lunched at the hotel and that a taxi was booked to convey them to the launch. It was quiet on Herm, the hotel manager told them, with a handful of charming little shops, the hotel and a pub. The island was small enough to enjoy walking—half a mile across and a bare mile and a half long, and there was the famous Shell Beach . . . He beamed at them, not knowing the aunts well enough to realise that they never walked more than a few years at a time. Prudence thought wistfully of an afternoon's exploring; out of the question with her elderly companions. All the same, the trip would be interesting.

The launch had been booked for eleven o'clock, and Pretty and Sieke left Prudence still at breakfast in order to get the aunts ready for that hour. It was still only nine o'clock. She drank the last of her coffee and wandered out across the courtyard and into the garden before the hotel. It was going to be a lovely day, and she perched on the side of a chair and admired the view. She didn't hear Jerome until he was beside her.

'What a heavenly morning!' she exclaimed, and smiled up at him. 'We're going over to Herm for lunch.'

'The launches will be pretty full,' he warned her.

'Oh, I've hired a launch just for us,' she explained. 'My aunts couldn't go otherwise. Have you been there? Is the White House a good hotel? We're lunching there.'

'Excellent, yes. I've been there several times. I would have enjoyed showing you the Shell Beach; there are some delightful walks too.'

'Yes, well . . . I don't suppose I shall have the chance to explore, but I'm looking forward to it all the same.'

'At least you'll go in comfort.' Jerome gave her a sharp glance. 'Not many people go to the expense of hiring a launch for themselves.' He saw her faint frown and went on smoothly, 'I don't suppose it occurs to them, and it's well worth it; the queues for the returning boats can be quite long towards the end of the afternoon.' He moved a little away. 'Well, I must have breakfast, I'm going over to Catel to see some friends.'

Mentioning friends gave him a more solid background, and Prudence said at once, 'Oh, how nice for you! You must know the island very well.'

'Like the back of my hand,' he said lightly. As indeed he did, for he came most years, staying at good hotels, seeking out the well-to-do, intent on what he jokingly thought of as heiress-hunting. This time, he thought smugly, it looked as though he might have found her. Obviously the darling of her aunts, good-looking as well, and what he had gleaned so far led him to believe that she was well heeled. Her clothes were expensive, too.

He ate a hearty breakfast, well content.

Herm was delightful; the aunts, fortified by coffee at the hotel, strolled round the few shops—a boutique selling charming clothes, a small pottery selling non-tourist glass and china, and an even smaller shop selling postcards, paperbacks and all the trifles which hotel clientele might need.

They made their purchases, gave Prudence a pretty scarf she had admired and went at their own pace back to the hotel, where they lunched in comfort. Prudence had taken the precaution of warning the manager that Mrs Wesley required a diabetic meal and had suggested a suitable menu, so that, confronted by the well-planned dishes which she was unable to take exception to, Aunt Beatrix was able to bear the sight of her companions enjoying a lobster with rich mayonnaise followed by an even richer Charlotte Russe.

They consented to rest after this, sitting in comfortable chairs in the shade of the garden, but Prudence's hope of going off by herself for an hour was doused by their suggestion that she should read aloud from the newspaper they had bought with them from the hotel. A suggestion from the aunts, however graciously put, was tantamount to an order from anyone else: Prudence opened *The Times* and began on the proceedings in Parliament, constantly interrupted by Aunt Emma, discoursing on the politics of her own country.

They had tea presently and then returned to the launch, where its owner sat, smoking his pipe. He had had a nice peaceful day with a good lunch at the pub, satisfied that he had made three times as much money as he usually did and had been able to take it easy at the same time. He handed the ladies into the boat and took them back to St Peter Port, taking care not to go at any speed, Aunt Beatrix having assured him that she was prone to seasickness.

There was a taxi waiting for them; Prudence had been instructed to ask the receptionist at the White House to phone over to Guernsey and arrange for one to meet them. Prudence had felt quite apologetic about it, but the aunts took it as a matter of course that their way should be smoothed for them. She surveyed them with affection as she accompanied them into the hotel. They had enjoyed their day, and despite their absorption in their own comfort they were quite incapable of being unkind to anyone. 'Delightful,' observed Aunt Beatrix, 'and they say it will be another splendid day tomorrow. Should we take a drive, do you think?'

At dinner that evening they discussed where they should go. 'Perhaps an afternoon outing?' suggested Prudence. 'You've had a long day, a rest tomorrow morning might be a good idea.'

They agreed. 'And perhaps you would go to the town, dear, and get that rather nice gold chain that we thought might do for dear Cordelia. I'll give you a cheque and my card, as I can't quite remember its cost.'

There had been no sign of Jerome. Prudence went to bed feeling vaguely let down, but he was having his breakfast when she went to the restaurant in the morning.

'Another lovely day,' he observed. 'Are you driving somewhere?'

'Not until this afternoon.' She helped herself to orange juice and sat down at her table. Sieke and Pretty had already breakfasted, and Jerome brought his coffee over and sat down opposite her with a friendly, 'May I?'

'I'm going into the town, I have to get something for my aunts. They're a little tired after yesterday.'

'They enjoyed themselves? And you?'

'Lovely, only I would have liked to see the whole island.'

He answered easily, 'Oh, well, I dare say you'll come again. Are you walking into town? May I go with you? I need to go to my bank.'

It would be pleasant to have company. They set out presently, after Prudence had visited the aunts and made sure that they were rested and had all they needed. Armed with an open signed cheque, she joined Jerome in the foyer.

They went up the hill this time, away from the sea, through Hauteville and then down the steps by the Town Church. It was still early and, although the streets were pleasantly filled, they weren't crowded.

'The bank can wait,' said Jerome. 'Suppose you do your shopping first.'

The jewellers was on the corner of the arcade, its windows glittering with gold and gems. Prudence went in and was instantly recognised as the young woman who had been in previously with the elderly lady who had liked a particularly expensive gold chain. It was produced for her now—a lovely thing of solid gold links. Jerome had come in with her, and she turned to him now.

'Pretty, isn't it?' she said. 'And very well made.' She turned back to the salesman. 'I'll take it, please. I have a cheque and my aunt's cheque card.'

She bent to write the cheque and Jerome, without appearing to do so, saw the amount—a very substantial sum, and paid without so much as a lift of the eyebrows. He wandered away and inspected some samples of silverware in another case. Only a few more days, he reflected, before they would leave, and although Prudence liked being with him he was clever enough to know that circumstances had thrown them together, not her choosing. He would have to go carefully, on the other hand he had very little time...

They left the shop and he suggested coffee. 'Yes, please,' said Prudence, 'but wouldn't you like to go to your bank first?'

'Yes, of course, just across the street here. I won't be
a moment—just to cash a cheque.'

He went inside, went to one of the desks and sat down,
picked up the pen and scribbled on the back of a paying-
in slip, just in case she had followed him in. But Prudence
was quite uncurious—besides, it was none of her
business. She crossed the street again and studied the
clothes in a boutique until Jerome joined her.

He took her to a small café at the far end of the high
street and then led the way back to the harbour. He made
no demur when she said she should be getting back, and
they walked the length of the boulevard and up the steep
hill to the hotel, where he bade her a friendly goodbye.
'A very pleasant morning,' he added. 'A pity you'll be
leaving in a few days. I do hope you'll let me have your
address in England; it would be nice to meet again some
time.'

He was clearly clever enough to keep away from her
for the rest of the day, but the following morning as she
strolled across the garden after breakfast he came
towards her. 'Off sightseeing?' he asked. 'Have you been
to the Rose Centre? It's well worth a visit, rather early
in the year, but all the same most interesting; your aunts
might enjoy it. It's quite easy to find...'

Prudence went to the car parked close by and got out
the map and spread it on the bonnet and together they
studied it. 'I'd be delighted...' began Jerome, then
stopped, aware that someone was standing beside him.

'Hello, Prudence,' said Haso.

She was furious with herself for blushing. It was shock,
she told herself, eyeing him warily, wishing him good
morning in a faint voice. But the look he bent upon her

was positively jovial. 'A splendid day,' he told her, and looked at Jerome.

'Oh, well—yes. This is Jerome Blake, he's staying here and has been kind enough to advise me about trips.' She looked at Jerome. 'This is Professor ter Brons Huizinga, from Holland,' she added unnecessarily.

The men shook hands and Haso said, still very friendly, 'I'm going to have breakfast before I see the aunts. I left quite early.'

'How did you come?' asked Prudence politely, a little uneasy because Jerome was so silent.

'Oh, I flew myself over. I'll leave you to tell the aunts I'm here, Prudence. Were you planning an outing with Mr Blake? Do go ahead; I'll spend the morning here with the aunts. We'll meet for lunch, shall we?'

He beamed at her and then at Jerome, rather like a benevolent uncle, and she seethed silently. The nerve of it, arranging the day to suit himself! He caught her fulminating look and his eyes danced with amusement. 'Enjoy yourselves,' he advised them with what she felt to be false kindness, then he turned and strolled away in the direction of the restaurant.

Jerome, beyond an odd word here and there, had taken no part in the conversation, but now he said, 'Has he got his own plane? He seems very young to be a professor. One of these brainy chaps, earning fabulous sums helping fools like me.'

Prudence was angry, she was upset too, and her feelings were hurt, although she hadn't had time to find out just why. She said snappily, 'Oh, he's clever, but he doesn't need to earn a living...'

She could have bitten her tongue out for saying that, but somehow Haso had made her feel foolish and, even worse, careless of his aunts' welfare.

Jerome was too clever to answer her, he said soothingly, 'Well, since you're free to do as you like this morning, shall we go along to the Aquarium? It's quite interesting, and we can follow the cliff path to Fermain Bay and have coffee there and take a bus back. Or we could take the car...?'

'No, I'd like to walk. Shall I meet you in half an hour—you might have to wait a bit.'

'I shan't mind that, Prudence.' He made his voice sound sincere and she went a little pink.

She put the map back in the car, locked it and went up to the aunts' rooms. They were delighted with her news, but she had expected them to be more surprised. Perhaps when you got old you didn't feel surprised any more. 'I dare say Haso will want to look you over,' she pointed out. 'He said he'd be up to see you when he had had some breakfast. He flew over this morning early.'

She went away to her own room to tidy herself and find a pair of sensible shoes and her shoulder-bag. Somehow the prospect of a morning in Jerome's company left her uninterested. She told herself not to be silly; it was a splendid chance to let Haso see that not everyone shared his dislike of her. She went back to Aunt Beatrix's room and found him there, sitting on the bed, eating a croissant.

He got up when she went in. 'There you are. Anything to tell me? I've seen Aunt Emma—she's splendid, and so, I imagine, is Aunt Beatrix.'

Prudence's sharp eyes had seen the croissant. 'Did that come up with your breakfast, Aunt Beatrix? You haven't eaten one?'

How awful if she had. After days of watching almost every mouthful Mrs Wesley had had, it would be just her bad luck for something to go wrong just as Haso had arrived. And why was he here, anyway?

'Don't panic,' said Haso softly. 'I took this off Aunt Emma's tray. I'm sure you've kept a watchful eye on both of them. Many thanks, Prudence.' His voice was bland. 'Now off you go and enjoy yourself with Mr—Blake.'

Prudence flounced to the door, but before she could go through it he added, 'I thought we might go out for dinner this evening, but if you want to spend an evening with—er—Mr Blake, I'm sure we shall all quite understand.'

She didn't answer, nor did she look at him, but closed the door with exaggerated care and went down to where Jerome was waiting for her.

His obvious pleasure at seeing her was balm to her ill-humour, but after a while she found herself becoming impatient at his rather fulsome compliments and the number of questions he asked about the aunts' homes and when he said with careful nonchalance, 'Your aunts—they seemed very distinguished ladies—from Dutch nobility, I dare say?' he was answered shortly.

'Yes—at least of the lesser sort. What made you ask?'

'I'm sorry, I must seem inquisitive, I don't mean to be. I meet many people on my travels and I'm deeply interested in people, especially of other countries.'

A reasonable answer, but it had grated on her ear. However, he laid himself out to be pleasant, and Prudence decided Haso's sudden appearance had made her edgy and peevish. She said suddenly, 'I'm sorry, I'm not much of a companion this morning.'

'I hope we're friends enough for that not to matter,' he told her, adding quickly, 'Have you seen Candie Gardens? They're delightful—we'll have coffee in Smith Street and go there if you like, it's only a short walk from the coffee house.'

The gardens were quite beautiful. They wandered round, stopping to examine the flowerbeds and admire the view out to sea, until Prudence said reluctantly that she had promised to be back for lunch.

Jerome took her through the old town, past the college and down Constitution Hill by the steps into Market Street, and then, since there was a little time to spare, led her through the market, between the stalls of fish and meat and vegetables, and in the flower market at the end of the building bought her a bunch of roses. She thanked him prettily, feeling a little uneasy at the proprietorial air he had suddenly adopted towards her. She had enjoyed his company, but she felt vaguely relieved that she would be saying goodbye to him in a few days. He was attentive, well mannered and most amusing, and yet there was something about him that she was uncertain about. She put the idea away from her and chatted a little too brightly to cover her uncertainty, but she found herself without words when they reached the hotel, and Jerome said with casual friendliness, 'You'll be too busy packing up tomorrow to spare time for me— would you come out to dinner this evening? There's a

delightful hotel—the Bella Luce—in Moulin Huet valley.
We can drive there—it's only a matter of three or four
miles. I believe you went that way with your aunts to
the pottery...'

'Yes, it's very pretty there.' Prudence hesitated, on
the point of refusing him nicely, when she saw Haso
striding towards them. There was a little smile lifting the
corners of his stern mouth and his eyebrows were raised
in what she felt sure was mockery of herself. She said
on an impulse, 'I'd love to come, thank you very much.
Where shall we meet?'

Haso was near enough to hear her. 'Why not the bar?'
he enquired genially.

Jerome said stiffly, 'Prudence is dining with me this
evening.'

'Splendid—there are some very good restaurants on
the island, so I'm told. Prudence, the aunts are in the
second lounge waiting for you. I'll collect them and see
you in the bar in ten minutes or so.' Haso turned to
Jerome. 'You must join us—I insist.' He bent a benevolent smile upon Jerome. 'Ten minutes suit you, too?'

He nodded and strolled away, and Prudence said, 'I'll
see you presently,' and made her escape to her room,
where she wasted five minutes of the ten sitting on her
bed wondering about Haso's excessive benevolence. She
came to the conclusion that he was making amends for
his rudeness.

It seemed as though she was right. In the bar, sitting
round one of the tables with the aunts and Jerome, he
became the genial host. It surprised her very much when
he started talking about his life in Holland. He said
nothing about his work as a surgeon, but he was more

than loquacious about the aunts' homes and went on at great length about his house.

'It's really a castle,' he explained, 'and full of treasures—of course, it costs the earth to maintain, but the family have had possession of it for hundreds of years. My aunts' homes are old too, and of course, the family own a good deal of land.'

Prudence could hardly believe her ears. This boastful Haso wasn't the man she knew. She glanced at the aunts to see if they had noticed anything, but they were sitting there, nodding their agreement and sipping their tonic water, looking so placid that she wondered if she had never known the real man Haso until now. She studied his face; it was quite bland and his voice offered her no clues, and she was very relieved when they went up to the restaurant, leaving Jerome to speak to some other guests.

Over lunch the aunts debated as to how they should spend their afternoon. 'If we're going out this evening I think you should rest until tea time,' suggested Haso. 'I have to go out, perhaps Prudence will keep you company?'

'Yes, of course. I'll finish the novel I've been reading to you—we can have tea in the lounge and have a game of Patience afterwards, if you would like that.'

'We'll go out about half-past seven,' said Haso. 'What time are you going, Prudence?'

She eyed him across the table. 'Jerome suggested about eight o'clock.'

'You're not going far?' he asked casually.

'No, but one can't go far anywhere on Guernsey.'

He made a non-committal answer and asked if Pretty and Sieke were enjoying themselves.

'I imagine so,' observed Aunt Emma vaguely. 'They like their lunch in the bar and I believe they breakfast here with Prudence. I don't know about dinner...'

'They have it here,' said Prudence, 'before we do.'

The aunts elected to rest in Aunt Emma's room; there was a chaise-longue upon which Aunt Beatrix allowed Prudence to make her comfortable, while her sister lay on the bed and Prudence sat between them. She began to read, but within twenty minutes or so gentle snores allowed her to close the book and stroll out on to the balcony to sit in the sun and do nothing.

She was getting lazy, she reflected, and used to the kind of carefree life which she was never likely to enjoy. She began to think about a job; in a few days she would be back in England and would have to look for work without delay. The thought was disturbing; hospitals and nursing seemed to be in another world. Perhaps she should never have accepted Aunt Beatrix's invitation in the first place. By now she would have been safely in Scotland or somewhere similar, running a ward efficiently and perfectly content—well, almost perfectly. But if she had done so she wouldn't have met Jerome. Or Haso.

She was aroused from these unhappy thoughts by Aunt Emma requesting a glass of water, and, since she was awake and felt like a chat, Prudence returned to her chair and listened patiently and with affection while her aunt made sweeping statements about politics, the world situation and education, which was her idea of a chat.

Prudence replied when necessary and allowed her thoughts
to wander, but somehow they always returned to Haso.

She wore the corn-coloured silk dress that evening,
and the pearls Mrs Wesley had given her on her eight-
eenth birthday, unaware that in Jerome's eyes she presented a picture of moneyed elegance. She looked
particularly lovely, for she had met Haso on her way—
the aunts, as so often happened, were hopelessly un-
punctual—and he had eyed her with one of his mocking
smiles. 'You look . . .' he hesitated, 'beautiful. Also well
heeled.'

Prudence said a little stupidly, 'Oh, but the pearls were
a present from Aunt Beatrix, and I spend far too much
money on clothes instead of saving it.'

He looked her up and down deliberately. 'Money well
spent, my dear—although you'd look good in a potato
sack. Have a lovely evening with your Mr Blake.'

'He isn't my Mr Blake, and you're being hateful
again!'

She swept past him, and when she saw Jerome, gave
him a dazzling smile; she might not be quite at ease with
him, but at least he didn't poke fun at her.

Jerome was no fool; he set about lulling her into a
sense of confidence in himself; he talked lightly of
nothing much as they drove to the hotel, and, when they
were there, sat her in the bar and kept the conversation
to generalities. The restaurant was nicely filled and they
had a table by a window with a splendid view. The meal
was delicious—cold watercress soup, followed by *poulet
à l'estragon* eaten with a fresh mushroom salad, and
strawberries and thick Guernsey cream. Jerome had
chosen a Muscadet, very dry and light, and the good

food and the wine eased away the last of Prudence's
vague feeling of disquiet. They had their coffee at the
table and then, since it was still light and a lovely evening,
they strolled into the grounds of the hotel. Jerome didn't
put a foot wrong—there had to be really the right
moment, but that wasn't yet; he looked at the pearls—
undoubtedly real—and the dress which certainly hadn't
come off the peg, and bided his time. He had sensed her
reluctance to spend the evening with him despite the
dazzling smile, and he thought he had overcome it.
Presently they got into the car and drove back to the
hotel, taking the small lanes and not hurrying.

It was almost eleven o'clock when they got out of the
car, and still pleasantly warm. 'I always think the view
at night over the harbour is something to remember.'
Jerome spoke casually, and Prudence strolled across the
grass to the low stone wall overlooking the bay, hardly
noticing when he joined her, for she was wondering if
the aunts and Haso had enjoyed their evening together;
the thought that she would have liked to have been with
them even if she had quarrelled with Haso swept everything else out of her head, so that she didn't quite take
in what Jerome was saying when he spoke. He sounded
serious and at the same time strangely urgent.

She turned to look at him in the dim light from the
hotel lamps. 'I'm sorry—I was thinking. What did you
say?'

It was annoying to have to repeat everything once
more. He gave a little laugh. 'Prudence, I'm in love with
you—I know we haven't known each other long, but
with me it was a case of love at first sight. Will you
marry me? I know I haven't much to offer you.' He had

never told her what he did for a living and he wasn't going to now, because in truth he did nothing, relying on a small inheritance and his wits. 'But money isn't important—besides, I have contacts, and with your money I could set myself up.' He added rather belatedly, 'We could be very happy.'

Prudence had listened to him, astounded, unable to utter a word, so that he took her silence for delighted surprise. When she gave a small, gasping laugh he put an arm round her. 'You must have known how I felt?'

'No, I didn't. What makes you think I have money, Jerome?'

'Your aunts...my dear girl, it sticks out a mile! Personal maids, special launches, and that Professor—their nephew, isn't he?—with his own plane—besides, he made no secret of the fact, did he? And you're their niece...'

She slid from his arm. 'But I'm not—I'm no relation—they're old friends of the family. I haven't any money at all, Jerome.'

He didn't believe her. 'Perhaps not now—but you're bound to get something...'

She stood looking at him, finding it hard to believe that their conversation was actually taking place; it sounded like a third-rate novel.

She said clearly in a cool voice, 'Jerome, shall we forget all this? You've been wasting your time. I think you wanted to marry me for my money, only I haven't any. You'll have to believe that, and even if I had I wouldn't marry you if you were the last man on earth.'

She turned away, and he put out an arm and swung her round. 'You're right, you've wasted my time, but I'll give you something to remember me by...'

He pulled her close and she said icily, 'Let me go, Jerome!'

He was too angry to listen, he dragged her closer, and she lifted her hand and slapped his face—a mistake, perhaps, because he swore and tightened his hold.

'If I were you,' said Haso from the darkness of the trees behind them, 'I should let the lady go. For one thing, she is no sylphlike creature to be easily crushed, and for another I would be constrained to make you.'

Jerome loosed his hold so smartly that Prudence almost lost her balance. She hadn't been particularly scared, and now she was furiously angry—Haso had made her sound like some muscular athletic type squeezed into size twenty! She wanted very much to go somewhere quiet and very dark and have a good cry. She said loudly, 'There's no need to do anything of the sort, Professor. Mr Blake must realise that to go away as quickly as possible is the only thing to do.'

'Go indoors,' said Haso in a soft voice that demanded instant obedience.

Prudence went without a word. The lounges and hall were empty, guests had either gone to bed or were still out in the town. She wandered round and round the wide hall, carefully not looking out into the dark garden. She could have gone to her room, but that would have been cowardly. Haso thought nothing of her, he would think even less if she ran away from him. It was none of his business, anyway, she thought crossly, and when a moment later he came in through the door she said so, giving him a defiant look. Temper had given her a splendid colour and she was breathing rather fast.

Haso leaned up against a marble stand holding a pot plant. 'No, I know—the Jeromes of this world are no match against you, Prudence, but since I met the fellow I've been wanting to knock him down.'

'Whatever for?'

'It's time you grew up, dear girl. He's an adventurer, on the look-out for easy money, and he thought he had found it. Had you fallen in love with him?'

'Me? In love with him?' Her voice was an indignant squeak. 'You must be joking!' Suddenly she wasn't angry any more, only forlorn. 'But it was nice to have someone to talk to and he—seemed to like me.' She stood in front of Haso. 'Something always goes wrong when I see you.' She added like a child, 'We had a lovely dinner.'

Somehow that was the last straw. She burst into tears.

CHAPTER SIX

FOR the second time in half an hour Prudence found herself in the arms of a man, but this time she made no attempt to free herself. On the contrary, she laid her head against Haso's massive shirt front and snivelled and gulped, while his great arms held her with a comfort which was reassuringly avuncular.

She wept for a minute or two until Haso released an arm to fish out a handkerchief and mop her face. 'Now blow,' he told her, and when she had done so, 'Feel better now?' He smiled very kindly at her woebegone face. 'Now come and sit down. I'm going to fetch us a drink.'

He steered her into the lounge and sat her down, leaving her alone in the quiet room. He was back within minutes, carrying a small tray. He set a glass on the table before her and said, 'Drink up.'

'What is it?'

'Brandy.'

'I never drink brandy.'

'There's always a first time. Drink up!'

Prudence took a sip and choked a bit. She looked into her glass and mumbled, 'Did you fight?'

He laughed. 'No, we had a talk. He won't bother you again, Prudence.' He gave her a searching look. 'It will be your last day tomorrow. I think we might take the aunts on a final tour of the island, don't you?' She nodded and took another sip of brandy, not looking at him.

'I'll see you on to the plane before I leave, but I dare say I'll be home before you. When do you want to go back to England?'

Clearly he would be glad to be rid of her. 'As soon as it can be arranged, please. Aunt Beatrix is staying on for a while, isn't she? She's quite used to her diet now and very good about taking her pills.'

'Good. Toss off that brandy and go to bed.' Haso searched her woebegone face; it was still lovely, despite a pink nose and puffy eyelids. 'It will be all right in the morning.' His voice was gentle.

She stood up and he got up, too. 'Goodnight, Prudence.'

'I—I haven't thanked you—I'm most grateful, and I'm sorry I cried...'

'Think nothing of it.' His smile was gentle, but she sensed impatience. She wished him goodnight and left him there.

She didn't sleep very well, but she went to breakfast pale but composed, hopeful that there would be few people in the restaurant. Only a handful, as it turned out, and that included Haso, sitting at her table, studying the menu. He got up as she reached him, wished her a placid good morning and beckoned to the waiter. 'Tea?' he asked her. 'I think we might have coffee in town. The aunts won't be ready much before half-past ten, and I want to buy a present for Mama—perhaps you would help me choose it?'

She was grateful to him for making it easy for her. 'Yes, I'd like tea and I'll willingly help you with the present.' She was sipping her orange juice. 'Have you anything in mind?'

'A piece of jewellery, perhaps. What are you eating?'

Prudence gave her order and buttered some toast. 'I bought a charming gold chain a few days ago—the aunts wanted it for your mother...' She stopped, while colour flooded her face. She stared down at her plate, remembering that Jerome Blake had been with her, and Haso, watching her, read her thoughts. He said quietly, 'Then it mustn't be a gold chain. She likes brooches.'

He led the talk to generalities, not appearing to notice that she hadn't much to say for herself, and when they had finished he said, 'We'll drive down, there should be somewhere to park at this time of day. Will ten minutes do for you to take a look at the aunts?'

She nodded, glad to have her morning arranged for her. The aunts were happily occupied in overseeing the packing of their clothes ready for the following day; Prudence went through the routine of checking their pulses, Aunt Emma's specially, and checked Aunt Beatrix's diet and pills, but really she wasn't needed any more. She found Haso outside the hotel, sitting on the wall which enclosed the lawn, smoking his pipe and reading *The Times*, and just for a moment she thought how nice and safe he looked. She wasn't quite sure what she meant by that; all she knew was that dislike had nothing to do with the feeling of being in a pair of safe hands.

He was a man who could find a place to park his car in without any fuss. They left it in the narrow side street and went to the jewellers where she had bought the gold chain. Prudence would have liked to have lingered at the windows, but he urged her inside and requested the saleswoman to show him some brooches, and when he was asked if he had any preference, simply said, 'Oh, diamonds, I think,' and then to Prudence, 'This is where I need your advice.'

Privately she considered that he was quite able to decide for himself, none the less she bent over the selection set before them. After a short time Haso said, 'Well?'

She poked gently at a diamond bow, a dainty trifle about an inch and a half across, set with diamonds in a ribbon pattern. 'I like this, but perhaps your mother has different tastes from mine.'

'I like it too, and I think she will. We will have it.'

The assistant went away to get a box in which to pack it, and Prudence wandered off, not wishing to be nosy about its price. It would be by no means cheap, of that she was quite sure.

They had coffee and then went in search of a pipe for Wigge and chocolates for the maids, and by then it was time—more than time—to return to the hotel and collect the aunts.

Haso drove them round the island and took them to lunch at La Frégate Hotel, tucked away on the far side of St Peter Port. Les Cotils was quiet and the hotel was dignifiedly quiet with a restaurant overlooking the sea and delicious French food. With an eye to Aunt Beatrix they chose *tomates suisses*, then jellied chicken with a green salad. Strawberries and cream rounded off their meal, although Aunt Beatrix, denied the cream, was inclined to be petulant. She was slightly mollified when

Haso lightly pointed out that she could have all the coffee she wished for.

After lunch he drove them to Cornet Castle, and after settling his aunts in chairs in a sheltered spot beneath the walls, he climbed up to the topmost viewpoint with Prudence, where they stood side beside each other, not speaking, watching the launches crossing and re-crossing to Herm and Sark.

Prudence hung over the wall to catch a glimpse of the aunts below.

'Have you been here before?' she asked.

'Several times. I've sailed over once or twice, but now I have the plane I can get here in an hour or two. I stay at La Frégate: no radio, no television, utter peace and quiet, but of course it would have been too hilly for the aunts. The de Havelet is pretty good, though.'

'We've been very comfortable, and it was pleasant for the aunts because they could sit outside in the garden and watch the harbour.'

He said abruptly, taking her by surprise, 'Blake went early this morning.'

How she hated herself for blushing, but she answered composedly enough. 'I was a bit scared of meeting him . . .'

She was even more surprised when he asked blandly, 'Do you suppose we are beginning to like each other a little?'

She said hesitantly, 'You've been very kind to me and I'm so grateful, really I am.'

'But it hasn't altered your opinion of me?'

'It's difficult to explain.' She turned to meet his look. 'I don't know you, do I? And whether I like you or not doesn't really matter—we're most unlikely to see each other again once I return to England, but I can have an opinion of you whether I like you or not. I think you're a kind man who takes good care of his family and his patients. I—I hope you'll be happy—you and Christabel—when you marry, living in your lovely home.'

She faltered then, because Haso was smiling his small mocking smile, his eyes hooded. 'What a pretty speech!'

Prudence turned away. 'You're impossible!' But after a few steps she stopped. 'I'm sorry, I didn't mean that, only you make me cross. I really do hope you'll be happy.'

He said gravely, 'You are a nice girl, Prudence. Why aren't you married?'

It was strange that he should annoy her so much, and within minutes it was forgotten. 'Aunt Maud is always asking me that...'

'And what do you tell her?'

She laughed a little. 'Why, that I'm waiting to be swept off my feet. I know that's silly—I'm not the right size or shape for that, but it must be marvellous to be showered with roses and diamonds and champagne. Not that it ever happens outside romantic novels.'

'No? Don't be too sure of that, Prudence. Now how about tea? Shall we go back to the hotel, or would the aunts enjoy it at one of the cafés?'

'Perhaps the hotel would be best, then Aunt Beatrix won't be tempted to eat cakes. You're pleased with them both?'

'Yes. Aunt Beatrix tells me that she intends staying in Holland for another week or two. Pretty will stay too, of course. But she and Aunt Emma should be all right now. They're remarkably tough, you know.'

They started back the way they had come, and found the aunts quite ready to return for their tea. And after that Prudence had no more chance of talking to Haso, for although they met at dinner the talk was general and no mention was made of their journey.

There was no hitch in the morning; the aunts were shepherded into the car and, with Prudence sitting beside him, Haso drove to the airport where he saw them as far as Passport Control, bade them goodbye, gave Prudence a rather casual nod and waited until they were out of sight. Prudence, taking a last look, resisted a strong urge to rejoin him, which, considering they had parted coolly, was ridiculous. In any case, she reminded herself, he would be returning to Holland that same day.

She took Aunt Emma's arm as they went on board and settled both ladies comfortably, a lengthy task, before sitting down herself on the opposite side of the gangway.

Aunt Beatrix wriggled majestically in her seat-belt. 'How fortunate that this is a short flight,' she observed in resonant tones. 'I really don't care for flying. I shall ask Haso to drive me back to England.'

'He might be too busy,' suggested Prudence.

'I'm sure he will find time for me, my dear. A few days in London would make a nice change for him and give him a rest from the van Bijl girl.'

There weren't many passengers, but those there were were listening avidly to Aunt Beatrix's observations. It was a good thing that the noise of the engines drowned whatever else she had had in mind to say. Prudence offered her a book, her special reading glasses and the smelling salts she refused to travel without. Aunt Emma wanted a cushion for her head and professed herself ready for a brief nap, but first she needed something to drink... They would be landing before the two ladies had had their needs satisfied; Prudence thought enviously of Pretty and Sieke, who Haso would have as passengers in his plane. She might have gone in their place, she thought peevishly, and they could have travelled in the plane with the aunts. If Haso had liked her enough he would have suggested that, she felt sure. As it was, here was another proof, if proof were needed, that he didn't like her.

She brooded about it for a little while and then dismissed it from her mind and concentrated on her plans for getting a job. The moment they were back she would ask Haso to arrange a flight for her to return to England, and if he showed a reluctance to help her then she would do it for herself.

Wim was waiting for them at Schiphol, transferring them and their luggage with practised ease to the car and then, driving at exactly the speed the aunts liked, transporting them back to Aunt Emma's house.

The household had assembled to meet them, and Prudence was surprised to see Pretty and Sieke waiting in the hall.

'Such a lovely trip,' said Pretty to Prudence. 'You've no idea, miss—landed in the doctor's grounds and got driven back here.' She sighed. 'I'll miss it all when we go back to London.' She eyed Prudence's pretty face. 'You too, miss?'

'Well, it's all a bit different, Pretty. I'll be glad to see my aunt again, though.'

'That's what the doctor said,' Pretty told her as she slid away to help with the various bags and wraps being brought in from the car.

Prudence went to her room and surveyed the cases Wim had already taken there. There wasn't much point in unpacking; she emptied her overnight bag and went downstairs again, just in time for Sieke to tell her she was wanted on the telephone.

Haso had wasted no time. 'You wanted to go back to England as soon as possible? I have to go to London the day after tomorrow—I'll give you a lift. Be ready to leave by nine o'clock in the morning, will you? I'm taking the car.'

He didn't wait for an answer. Prudence stared at the receiver in her hand frowning fiercely. 'Well, of all the rude, arrogant men!' She replaced the receiver and the phone rang again before she could take her hand away. She picked it up, her 'Hello' icy. If he was going to apologise, he had better make it very civil. A woman's voice, speaking very strongly accented English.

'Professor ter Brons Huizinga wishes me to regret that he could not finish his conversation; he was requested most urgently in the operating theatre.'

Prudence said 'Thank you,' and, since the voice had no more to say, hung up again. It was Haso's fault, of course; he made so light of his work that one tended to forget that he did any. Rather put out, she went off to see if the aunts needed her, and at once became immersed in the search for one of Aunt Emma's diamond ear-rings which had unaccountably disappeared, to be found presently, lodged in her hair.

There was no sign of Haso the next day, although Christabel arrived during the afternoon. The aunts were still resting, so it fell to Prudence's lot to entertain her. Not that there was much entertaining necessary; it was soon obvious to her that Christabel had come to discover exactly what Haso had done while he was in Guernsey, and since Prudence gave her only bare bones of news about their activities there, she gave up her questions presently and said sweetly, 'Haso was so glad to get home—he does miss me so much if he has to go away. It I hadn't been in Italy I would have gone with him. We do so much together, you know.' She shot Prudence a sly glance. 'It's so important really to know each other before marriage, don't you agree?'

'I dare say,' Prudence managed to sound offhand, 'although I don't see any point in waiting around once one has made up one's mind.' She added naughtily, 'Perhaps Haso hasn't made up his.'

Christabel went red. After a pregnant pause she said, 'I hear you are returning to England tomorrow.'

'Yes,' said Prudence cheerfully. 'Haso's giving me a lift—but of course he would have told you that.'

It was only too evident from Christabel's face that he had done no such thing. She said stiffly, 'Haso has been at the hospital since he got back—he is a very important man, you know. We shall see each other this evening.'

Prudence was feeling reckless. 'Why don't you come to England too?'

'Quite impossible; I have several engagements I cannot cancel.'

'You lead a busy life?' asked Prudence innocently. 'You have a job?'

The other girl gave what in anyone else would have been termed a sniff.

'Certainly not! I have no need to have one, but I have many friends and a full social life.'

Prudence nodded. 'It must be exhausting,' she observed, still very innocent. 'Of course, when you marry, you'll have to give that up, I suppose?'

'Certainly not. Haso has no need to work; he will retire . . .'

'Now you do surprise me, although I expect one should be prepared to sacrifice a good deal for someone one loves.'

Prudence smiled kindly at the somewhat discomfited Christabel, feeling that she had at least kept up her own end. All the same, it was a relief when Aunt Beatrix came in. She greeted Christabel with chilly politeness, sat down and asked, 'Are you stopping for tea? My sister will join me in a moment. Prudence, will you ring for Wim?'

Christabel declared that she had to get back. 'Haso will be expecting me,' she explained coyly. She made her goodbyes prettily, adding to Prudence, 'We are not likely to meet again, I think, but I am sure that if there is news of you, Mevrouw ter Brons Huizinga will tell me.'

Prudence said benignly, 'Oh, I'm positive that nothing I do will be of interest to you—not once I'm back in England.'

When Christabel had gone, Aunt Beatrix observed thoughtfully, 'You dislike each other, you and Christabel? Of course, she is jealous. She has been so sure of Haso and now she has met you she is filled with doubt.'

Prudence busied herself with the tea-things. 'She has no need to be! Haso and I don't get on at all, you know.'

Aunt Emma had her mouth open to speak when her sister said smoothly, 'Oh, well, it would be a dull world if we all liked each other. I will take a slice of that chocolate cake, my dear. Are you ready to leave in the morning? We shall miss you very much, you have been so kind and caring of our needs. You must come again...'

'I shall be working,' said Prudence cautiously.

'Then you must come and stay with me,' declared Mrs Wesley. 'We will go to the theatre and visit art galleries together.'

The talk became general, and presently Prudence wandered off into the garden. It looked delightful, and she wished she could have seen the gardens at Haso's home just once more and said goodbye to his mother.

She strolled back to the house and found that lady sitting in the drawing-room with her aunts, which delighted her so much that she hurried forward to say, 'Oh, Mevrouw ter Brons Huizinga, I'm so glad to see you— I was only just now wishing I could say goodbye.'

'You return so quickly, my dear, and there has been so little time. But I hope it is not goodbye, only *tot ziens*. I would like you to see the gardens in a month's time— they will be beautiful...'

'I'd like that too, but I really do have to get a job.'

'Yes, I understand that and I hope you will find something to your liking.' She got up. 'Well, I must go back home. Haso will be here in the morning. Such a pity that he has appointments in London and that he will have no time to visit your Aunt Maud.' She sighed. 'He works too hard.'

She kissed Prudence, embraced Beatrix and Emma and went out to the car where Wigge was waiting for her. As he opened the door Mevrouw ter Brons Huizinga turned to Prudence. 'I hear that Christabel came this afternoon. I thought she would.' She nodded her elegantly coiffed head, then got into the car and was driven away, and Prudence, watching the car disappear through the drive gates, felt regret because she wouldn't see her again.

Prudence got up early the next morning, had breakfast, had a quick breath of air in the garden and went to say goodbye to the aunts; a protracted business while they reiterated their thanks, renewed their wish to see her again as soon as possible and handed her several small packages.

'For dear Maud,' said Aunt Beatrix, 'with our love—and these are for you, Prudence. Have a safe journey—dear Haso is such a good companion.'

A remark which Prudence accepted with reservations. With a final kiss she went downstairs to the hall. It was almost nine o'clock, and she intended to start off the day well, whatever happened to the rest of it.

Haso was in the hall, sitting on the edge of the wall table, drinking coffee and talking to Pretty, but he put his cup down when he saw Prudence and went to take her parcels.

'Good morning. You look like a Christmas tree. You're ready?'

'Quite ready. Could these go in the boot?'

He nodded, dropped a kiss on Pretty's gratified cheek and led the way out to the car. Wim was there, so was Sieke, and Prudence was touched at the kindness of their goodbyes. They both called 'Tot ziens' too as she got into the car beside Haso, and she turned and waved as he drove away from the house. Regret washed over her at leaving, but she was a sensible girl, she dismissed the nebulous thoughts that filled her head and asked briskly, 'Whereabouts do you want to drop me off? If you're going straight to London, perhaps you wouldn't mind going to Waterloo. I can pick up a train...'

'Near Tisbury, isn't it? I'll take you there.'

'Oh, well—but what about whatever you were going to do in London?'

'That's the day after tomorrow. I'll have time to kill.'

'That's kind of you, but there's no need.'

'None at all. We're catching the night ferry from Vlissingen; it will get us to Sheerness early in the morning and we should be at home by midday.'

After that he had little to say until they stopped for coffee, and then they only talked trivialities. Prudence, sustaining a tepid conversation, was glad when they drove on, for sitting silent in the car was far less awkward than facing him over a café table.

They reached the terminal with barely ten minutes to spare, so that once Haso had got their cabin tickets they drove on board. There weren't a great many cars in the vast deck. He took out their overnight bags and led the way up to the reception desk, got their keys and saw her to her cabin. 'I'll meet you by the Purser's office in ten minutes,' he told her. 'We'll have a meal before the restaurants get too busy. Do you want anything from the duty-free shop? Sherry for Aunt Maud, perhaps?'

He wandered away, and Prudence took a few things out of her overnight bag, did her face, combed her hair and went back to the Purser's office. Haso was there, standing at one of the windows watching Vlissingen slide away into the deepening dusk. He said as she joined him, 'You have been this way before? I prefer the hovercraft, but driving to Calais takes up too much time. Flying is the best way, of course, but I need the car...'

'Because of me? I do hope not?' She was feeling suddenly guilty.

'No. I am going to Birmingham before I come back. Shall we go in?'

The food was good, and Haso, whatever his secret feelings about her might be, was an excellent host. Prudence, quite forgetting that they didn't like each other, readily consented to stroll round the deck before she went to her cabin, indeed she so far forgot herself as to tell Haso that Christabel had been to see her.

They were standing at the rail watching the distant lights on the horizon. Haso didn't say anything for a few moments. 'To wish you goodbye?' he asked casually.

'Well, yes,' explained Prudence chattily; she was finding it so much easier to talk to him in the semi-dark and fortified by the excellent wine they had had with dinner. 'And to warn me off.'

Haso said softly, 'Oh, really—why was that?'

His voice was so gentle that she went on happily, 'Oh, she had the ridiculous idea that I was taking up too much of your interest. So silly!'

'Indeed, yes.' His voice was silky. 'And even sillier of you to imagine such a thing happening.'

With horrid clarity she recalled what she had said. She said waspishly, 'My imagination doesn't stretch so far. The mind boggles...'

She couldn't see his face, but his laughter sounded mocking. 'I think we had better say goodnight, Prudence, but before you go, do tell me one thing. If you had been taking up too much of my interest, would you have liked that?'

'That's a hypothetical question and doesn't need an answer. Goodnight.'

She turned to go, but he caught her by the shoulders and turned her round to face him. 'This won't need a answer either,' he said, and kissed her on her surprised mouth.

He had done it to annoy her, she assured herself as she got into her bunk, quite prepared to lie awake and get into a rage just thinking about it, but she had to admit that she had enjoyed it; she was still thinking about it when she fell asleep...

They met in the restaurant for breakfast, half an hour before the ferry was due to dock, and if Prudence had expected to feel awkward she had no need; Haso wished her a cheerful good morning, advised her to eat up without waste of time and applied himself to bacon and eggs. And, true enough, there was only just time to finish their meal before they were required to go down to the car deck and disembark, so that conversation was unnecessary and time-consuming. The business of going through Customs and Passport Control was quickly done; within fifteen minutes they were driving through

the uninspiring town of Sheerness and then the flat, dull
fields beyond, until after some time the Kent countryside presented its pretty face. But that was lost again as
they flashed up the motorway, circumvented London to
the south and joined the M3 to take, after some time,
the A303. The Daimler made light of the distance and
Haso drove fast in a calm, almost lazy fashion.
Prudence, busy with her thoughts, had long since given
up attempts to hold a conversation; it seemed to her that
they were turning off on to the narrow country road to
Tisbury in no time at all. She should have felt pleasure
at that, but she was conscious of disappointment that
the drive had seemed so short and that they had had so
little to say to each other and what they had said had
been hardly friendly. She remembered his kiss and
blushed.

'Why are you blushing?' asked Haso hatefully.

'I'm not. You need to turn off here and go through
Hatch...'

'Yes, I know. I looked it up on the map.'

She held her tongue with difficulty; after all, he had
driven her all the way to her home. He could just as
easily have left her at Waterloo station.

The village, when they reached it, looked charming.
Old Mrs Giles, stomping along the road to the post
office, saw them, recognised Prudence and stopped to
wave, and, as they passed the pub, Mr Grubb the
landlord was at the bar door taking a breath of air. He
waved, too. It was lovely to be home, thought Prudence,
refusing to admit to herself that the pleasure was tinged
with regret.

Aunt Maud was at the open door as Haso stopped the car, and she trotted over to put her head through the window. 'Darling, how lovely to see you again!' She beamed at Prudence, planted a kiss on her cheek and turned her attention to Haso.

She eyed the vast man sitting quietly, smiling a little, and said in tones of deep satisfaction, 'So you're Haso. How very nice!' She put out a hand and had it engulfed in one of his. 'Come in—lunch is just about ready. You're staying the night, of course—your room is ready for you.' If she heard Prudence's quick, indrawn breath, she made no sign.

'Thank you, Miss Rendell. I should like to stay until tomorrow morning. Where can I put the car?'

Prudence had got out and was standing uncertainly while her aunt directed Haso round the side of the house. 'There's a barn there—Prudence's Fiat is in it, but there's plenty of room.'

He got into the car again and drove away, and Aunt Maud put an arm around Prudence. 'What a very nice young man,' she commented, 'and how kind of him to bring you back.'

'He had to come to London anyway,' said Prudence, so sharply that her aunt looked at her.

'Yes—well, dear, it was thoughtful of him, just the same. Come indoors, I'll put the lunch on the table while you tidy yourself. I've put Haso in the room overlooking the garden at the back.'

Watching the Daimler disappear down the lane the next morning, Prudence told herself she was glad to see the last of Haso; he had been charming to Aunt Maud, patiently related all the news of his aunts, passed on the kind messages from his mother and presented her with two bottles of excellent sherry. Moreover, when she had suggested that if he should come to England again, he might like to visit her, he agreed to do so with flattering readiness. But his manner towards herself left much to be desired, she considered; he had been casual and at the same time quite sickeningly polite. His goodbyes had been brief with no mention of their meeting again.

Prudence went back into the house and began to clear the breakfast things ready for Winnie, the elderly woman who came each day to 'do' for Aunt Maud. Aunt Maud, sitting by the window looking through her post, looked up as she went in. 'The house seems empty now Haso has gone. I like him.' And, since Prudence didn't give more than a mumble in reply, 'You didn't find a man to sweep you off your feet while you were in Holland, dear?' she asked placidly.

Prudence thumped a tray-load of china down by the sink. 'No—no roses or champagne or jewels, and no serenades.' She sighed. 'Perhaps I'd better take up with Walter again.'

Aunt Maud said with ill-concealed satisfaction, 'He's found another girl, dear. Remember Marcia Greenaway—old Mrs Vine's great-niece?'

'She has glasses and wears the most frightful clothes...'

'Yes, dear. She also has money.'

Prudence sat down on the kitchen table and swung her very nice legs.

'Oh, well, I'll have to carve a career for myself, won't I?'

'That reminds me—there was a letter for you. It came yesterday, so I didn't send it on—somewhere in Scotland.'

A post she had applied for and forgotten because no one had replied. Now it seemed they were only too anxious to have her. Aberdeen seemed a long way away, but the job was a good one—Sister in charge of the women's surgical floor. She remembered how disappointed she had been when she had heard nothing after she had applied for it, and now she had the chance of getting it she felt no interest in it at all.

Her visit to Holland had unsettled her. If she had refused Mrs Wesley's invitation she wouldn't have felt so unsettled—she wouldn't have met Haso either. It was surprising to her that she thought of him so much, since they had never become friends. She sighed so long and loudly that her aunt, sitting close by at her writing-desk, turned to give her a searching glance. Quite obviously Mrs Wesley's plans concerning Prudence and Haso hadn't been successful. Perhaps, thought Aunt Maud, something could be done about that, given the opportunity. She sent up a fervent prayer, rather muddled, but to that effect, and, being a lady with a strong belief in the powers of the Almighty, nodded with a feeling of satisfaction when the phone rang, and it was Haso's voice at the other end.

She listened to what he had to say. He had had a phone call from Aunt Beatrix begging him to get Prudence to go to the flat. She had decided to stay a few more weeks with her sister, and she was concerned that the flat might be neglected. If Prudence would be so kind as to contact the cleaning lady and see that the place was aired and dusted . . .

Aunt Maud passed on this news with a pleased smile, but Prudence frowned. 'Why didn't she telephone me instead of Haso?'

'I really don't know, my dear. He kindly offers to come for you and drive you up to the flat—he'll be in London for a few more days. He wants to know at once so that he can reassure Aunt Beatrix.'

'I'm going to accept that job in Aberdeen,' said Prudence, a remark which appeared to have no bearing on the matter in hand, but which Aunt Maud understood very well.

'Yes, dear, but you could answer the letter when you get back—I dare say that whatever Aunt Beatrix has in mind can be dealt with in a day or two at the very most.'

Reasonable enough. 'All right, I'll go, then. When?'

Aunt Maud picked up the receiver. 'This evening, dear, about six o'clock.'

There was one thing Prudence had learned about Haso, if he said six o'clock he meant just that; she was ready and waiting with her overnight bag when he drew up silently before the front door. They were away within ten minutes, his regretful refusal to stop for coffee mitigated by the kiss he planted on Aunt Maud's cheek. 'I'll drop Prudence off the day after tomorrow on my way to Birmingham.' He waved and drove off without further comment.

'If you're going to Birmingham,' declared Prudence, 'you'll be miles out of your way. I'll come back by train.'

'I shall bring you back, so don't let's argue about it, my girl.'

'I'm not your girl!' snapped Prudence, and, following a train of thought asked, 'How's Christabel?'

'As beautiful as ever.' He added blandly, 'We should be in town soon after eight o'clock. I'll see you into the flat and come back in half an hour—I've booked a table for dinner at the Connaught.'

'I'm not wearing the right clothes—besides, I like to be invited, not told.' Here he was annoying her already, and they hadn't been ten minutes on the way.

He slowed to give her a good look. 'Just right for the Grill Room.' He held her look for a moment and she went pink. She had indeed spent some time and thought as to what to wear; the coffee-coloured crêpe-de-Chine outfit she had decided upon was charming, just right for a summer evening in town. She glanced with deep satisfaction at her shoes—Raynes and a wicked extravagance. Tomorrow, she reflected, she would find time to do a little shopping. She had brought only a cotton skirt and top with her, not suitable for shopping in town— or going out to lunch with Haso? said a little voice at the back of her head. Prudence dismissed the thought with a frown; dinner would be bad enough.

They made good time, and Haso saw her into the flat before driving off with the reminder that he would be back within half an hour. The flat looked pristine; well dusted and polished, and someone had left milk, bread, and eggs in the fridge. She supposed Aunt Beatrix had forgotten the arrangements she had made with the cleaning lady. Prudence put her things in the bedroom and went to the telephone. Mrs Briggs was at home and said that yes, of course she would come in the morning, and was there anything special?

Prudence explained, and arranged with Mrs Briggs to have a chat in the morning—before ten o'clock, she had added, with a thought to her shopping.

She had time to do her face and hair before Haso returned. She was hungry by now, and since she was to be given a good dinner she promised herself that she would do nothing to annoy him. She greeted him, therefore, with a sweet smile, offered him a drink, which he refused, and accompanied him out to the car, fortunately unaware of his secret amusement.

CHAPTER SEVEN

PRUDENCE had to admit that the splendid dinner which Haso gave her was well worth her efforts to be a perfect companion. Tarte Valentoise, hot from the oven, the Gruyère cheese, blending just so with the tarragon mustard, made an excellent hors d'oeuvre, pâté de saumon, served with shrimp sauce, followed by fillets of lamb accompanied by a fresh tomato puree and tiny potatoes, and all washed down by Chablis Grand Cru.

It seemed a pity not to sample the dessert Haso recommended. Soufflé aux marrons was, she had to admit, out of this world. Haso, contending himself with the cheeseboard, agreed that he had noticed that most women liked it, a remark which somehow rather spoilt her enjoyment of it.

Still, she was determined to maintain her role of agreeable companion; she listened attentively to all that he had to say, made only the most innocuous remarks if asked to give her opinion and in general behaved so unlike her usual self that the gleam of amusement in Haso's eyes became very pronounced. And when he took her back to the flat and she paused at the entrance to thank him for her delightful evening he listened to her little speech with a faint smile.

'Delightful, but surely hard work for you, Prudence, biting back the tart remarks I've come to expect from you and drinking in every word I uttered like a teenager at a pop concert. I dare say if I'd switched over to Latin it would have been all the same to you.'

She glared at him. 'You're beastly; quite the nastiest man I've ever met! I hope I never have to see you again!' Her voice, despite her best efforts, had become regrettably shrill.

'In that case, let us say goodbye, by all means.' He bent quickly and kissed her hard, turned on his heel and left her standing alone in the empty hall. She stood looking at the closed door for a few moments, then went up to Mrs Wesley's flat, where she sat down on one of the opulent sofas and had a good cry. Because she was so very angry, she told herself, and how dared he kiss her like that? She stopped being angry for a minute or two while she pursued the interesting thought that Christabel wouldn't have liked it at all—a chaste peck on the cheek was probably all Haso was allowed. 'And served him right,' said Prudence loudly, and fell to wondering why he had kissed her.

It wasn't until the next morning, sitting waiting for Mrs Briggs, that she realised she would have to find her own way back to Aunt Maud's the next day. It really had been a final goodbye last night, although Haso might come round to apologise. Unlikely, she decided as she went to admit Mrs Briggs.

Over coffee, sitting at the kitchen table, they discussed the members of Mrs Briggs' family at length, agreeing that the windows should be cleaned and the sweep booked before Mrs Wesley returned. Prudence made sure that Mrs Briggs was receiving her wages weekly from her aunt's solicitor and that she would continue to go to the flat twice a week, then she bade the lady goodbye before locking the door after her and embarking on a morning's shopping. It was surprising how quickly the paucity of her wardrobe was borne in upon her once she entered Harrods' doors, and as usual, she spent rather more than she could afford, reassuring herself with the fact that she would be working again in the near future. She bore her parcels back to the flat after a sketchy lunch, then made tea and tried everything on. Repacking the things neatly, she remembered that she would have to carry them all as well as her overnight bag, although she would get a taxi to Waterloo and another one at Tisbury, both of which would make further inroads into her depleted purse. She wandered into the kitchen and examined the contents of the fridge; unlike the previous evening, she would have to cook her own meal.

She was doing a final check of the flat before she left the next morning when the doorbell rang. There was a young man on the doormat with an envelope in his hand. He thrust it at her and said awkwardly, 'My name's Ted Morris—in the Professor's team, you know. He asked me to give you this.'

He had an ingenuous face and a thatch of red hair, and she liked the look of him. 'I'm just leaving, but come in while I read it, will you?'

She wondered why Haso had written to her, and opened the envelope a little impatiently. If it was an apology, he was wasting his time...

The note inside was brief and businesslike, informing her that the bearer would drive her back to Aunt Maud's house, adding unforgivably, that it was hoped she would be civil to the boy and not make difficulties.

Prudence swallowed powerful rage. 'You know Professor ter Brons Huizinga?'

'Well, as I told you, I'm in his team—I'm only a houseman.' He beamed at her. 'But I live in Wiltshire and it's my weekend off...if you don't mind?'

'How very nice of you. I was dreading the train journey. You're sure it's not taking you too much out of your way?'

Her smile made him her slave. 'Good lord, no—only a mile or so, it'll be nice to have your company. I'd do anything for the Professor—he's a splendid man; we don't see nearly enough of him.'

'What a shame,' observed Prudence warmly and mendaciously. 'I'm all ready to leave—unless you'd like a cup of coffee?'

'I'd rather get on, if you don't mind—I'll just about get home for lunch if we go now.'

He picked up Prudence's bag and she locked the door behind them. 'Where do you live in Wiltshire?' she asked.

'Just outside Warminster.'

In the car he confided that his free weekend was a surprise. 'I'm not due for another couple of weeks, but the Professor said he'd have to come back in three weeks, and he'd like me there.' Out of the corner of her eye she saw him swell with pride. He could be right, of course, but be that as it may, she thought she detected Haso's manipulating hand in the turning of events to suit himself. And anyway, she reflected pettishly, he had taken her wish never to see him again seriously. The thought gave her singularly little satisfaction.

Ted drove well, and it was still early in the day. They made good time, stopped for coffee at Fleet and sped on down the motorway to the A303, turning off to go through the charming village of Hindon and so to Tisbury and presently to Aunt Maud's house, and in that time Prudence had heard a great deal about Haso. It seemed he specialised in abdominal surgery and was a very respected surgeon, already with some international fame. And a splendid teacher, concluded Ted enthusiastically. Prudence, murmuring suitably at intervals, came to the conclusion that she hadn't known the real Haso at all. Not that that mattered, she reminded herself. She had turned the page on him and his rudeness.

Ted refused more coffee, declaring that his mother would be expecting him. He bade Aunt Maud goodbye, shook hands with Prudence and hoped to see her again, then took himself off, leaving Prudence to explain why Haso hadn't brought her back.

'I think he must have been busy,' she said carefully, 'but it was awfully kind of him to get Ted to drive me down.'

'Perhaps he'll find time to come and see us before he returns to Holland.'

'Most unlikely,' declared Prudence, so sharply that her aunt gave her a thoughtful look.

It was very nice to be back home. Prudence unpacked her overnight bag and spent the rest of the day tidying away the clothes she had had no time to see to before she had gone to London. That very evening she sat down and wrote to the hospital in Aberdeen, if she was still wanted she would have to set about getting references and even go for an interview if that was required. It was rather a long way away, and suppose she didn't like it when she was given the job? She reminded herself with some scorn that it would be a challenge and it was about time that she started doing an honest day's work again. That night, just before she slept, she found herself re-

calling Haso's home with something very like home-
sickness. It took quite an effort to concentrate on the
new job in Aberdeen.

The next day, with the letter posted, she felt better,
now she had something definite to look forward to. With
commendable zeal she turned out her wardrobe and
drawers, washed and ironed and mended, helped around
the house, shopped for her aunt and drove her on several
visits to friends. Most of Aunt Maud's friends were elderly, as was to be expected, and Prudence, sitting in a
variety of drawing-rooms, patiently answered kindly
questions about her work and thinly veiled ones as to
when she was going to marry and whom. These were
usually followed by arch references to Walter, who, it
seemed, to her surprise, hadn't told anyone that he and
she were no longer to be married. She was careful to
answer politely, for the questions were meant well and
she had known most of the questioners all her life, but
their questions set up a train of thought which she was
hard put to dispel. She was, after all, twenty-five, half-
way to thirty—suppose she never met a man she wanted
to marry?

She had an answer to that a few days later. On the
day that she had received a letter from Aberdeen offering her the post she had applied for. She had been
down to the village to Mrs Legg's to buy some stamps
and a few odds and ends for Aunt Maud and happily
had a gossip, although the gossip was mostly on Mrs
Legg's part; she thrived on it. Prudence went in through
the side door, down the passage to the kitchen, put her
purchases on the kitchen table and crossed the hall to
the sitting-room. Aunt Maud had gone to the Manor to
Mrs Vine, to visit her as she had taken to bed with ar-

thritis, and Ellen and the daily woman were upstairs having what they called their weekly turn-out.

It was a fine morning, the doors to the garden were open and the room was cool, smelling faintly of furniture polish and the pot-pourri which Aunt Maud made for herself each year. There was also somebody in it— Haso! Standing with his back to the room, looking out on to the garden.

He turned round as Prudence went in and stood looking at her, saying nothing, and she stared back for what seemed aeons of time—in fact a mere few seconds, but time enough for her to discover something. It hit her with all the force of a shower of cold water and the shock just left her without breath. Here was the man she wanted to marry, and why had it taken her so long to discover it? Her eyes searched his face, calm and expressionless but with lines of fatigue etched deep. Her instincts was to rush to him and fling herself into his arms, but common sense held her back, and a good thing too.

'I am here on my mother's behalf.' His voice was chillingly impersonal. 'She's very ill—a totally unexpected appendix followed by peritonitis. She's in hospital, but wishes to return home. Above all, she wishes for you to nurse her.'

Prudence took a few steps towards him and then stopped. 'Oh, Haso, I'm awfully sorry; she's such a dear...but why me?' She added a little wildly, 'Anyway, I can't—I've just accepted a post in Scotland—they wrote today.'

'Which hospital?'

'The Royal General in Aberdeen.'

She watched him cross the room to the telephone and pick up the receiver. She listened unbelievingly as he dialled a number, then asked, 'The Royal General? Put me through to the Principal Nursing Officer, please.' And then, 'It's Professor ter Brons Huizinga here—Miss Thursby? I've a favour to ask of you. I believe that you have accepted a Miss Prudence Makepeace for a Sister's post. Can it be cancelled?' There was a pause while he listened. 'Urgent family reasons. My mother is seriously ill and has set her heart on being nursed by Miss Makepeace. Yes—a matter of a fifty-fifty chance—peritonitis; I'm very worried indeed.'

Prudence opened her mouth several times to interrupt. She had just formulated a suitably quelling remark when he went on, 'You will? My everlasting thanks. I believe I have a consultation at your hospital in about a month's time—I shall express my thanks to you then.'

He put down the receiver. 'That's settled. How long will it take you to pack?'

She gaped at him. 'What do you mean?' She loved him, of that she was quite sure now, she would go through fire and water for him, but she would not be bullied. 'Pack?'

'Don't waste time, Prudence. I'm not asking you to do me a favour, I'm asking for my mother. I'm only too well aware of your opinion of me, but for my mother I am prepared to go to any lengths. She's very ill and she asks for you. I've cancelled your appointment at the Royal General and I'm taking you back to Holland with me. I'm asking you to come—as a nurse, Prudence. My mother likes you, I believe you may be able to give her the help she needs to recover.'

His voice was still cold and expressionless; it must have cost him something to have sought her out. She longed to go to him and put her arms around him and tell him that she loved him—something quite impossible. Instead she said quietly, 'Very well, I'll come. May I have half an hour to pack and phone Aunt Maud? She's over at the Manor.'

'Shall I drive over and bring her back?'

She was already at the door. 'That would help. How long should I be gone for?'

Haso said bleakly, 'That rather depends, doesn't it?' He had followed her to the door. 'We shall know within a few days, but shall we say two to three weeks? She is most unhappy in the hospital, I believe she may do better once she's home.'

They went their separate ways, and presently, as Prudence was packing, Aunt Maud joined her. 'Darling, how fortunate that Haso reached you before you'd gone to that job! Poor Cordelia—such a dear woman, and he is so devoted. Ellen is getting a quick meal—sandwiches and coffee, for you both. I believe he plans to fly back this afternoon. He flew over and hired a car to get here.'

Prudence was still trying to put first things first. Never mind that she fallen in love, she had to pack sensibly, remember her passport and her money, answer Aunt Maud coherently and remember to treat Haso with a cool sympathy and be willing to do exactly what he wanted. Afterwards, in the unforeseeable future, she would have time to sort out her own problems. Her mind shied away from them and she concentrated on listening to Aunt Maud's gentle voice. 'One case, dear? I don't suppose you'll wear aprons or something while you're nursing Cordelia.'

'Well, Haso will have to get them for me; I haven't any. Aunt Maud, I'm so sorry to dash off like this, but really I had no choice...'

'Of course not, dear. What's to happen to your job in Aberdeen?'

'Haso cancelled it—without telling me first.'

'His mother must really be very ill,' observed Aunt Maud.

Prudence slammed the case shut. 'And Haso is very ruthless. What about me and my future?'

Aunt Maud studied her neatly shod feet. 'Well, we'll have to see, won't we, dear?'

Haso was standing at the sitting-room windows, staring out at the garden. His 'There your are,' Prudence considered totally undeserved; she had been exactly twenty-five minutes, but because her heart ached for the weariness in his face, she said nothing, only went to the tray on the side-table and poured their coffee.

'You'd better eat something,' she told him briskly, 'then we shan't need to stop on the way.'

He smiled at that. 'I hadn't intended to do so, but you're quite right.'

Their brief meal over, they went out to the car, an elderly Ford, bade Aunt Maud goodbye, and drove off. And if we get to Heathrow under four hours in this old crock, I'll eat my hat! thought Prudence.

However, they weren't going to Heathrow. She discovered quickly enough that he was heading for Shaftesbury, and then remembered that he flew his own plane. There was a small airfield to the south of the town; he would have landed there. She was right; he skirted the town when they reached it and took the Blandford road, to turn off after a mile or so, taking the narrow road along the top of the hill until they reached the airfield.

All that while he hadn't spoken. Now he got out first, opened the door for her and got her case and said, 'Wait here, will you?'

The car was handed back and he picked up her case. 'The plane is over there.' He nodded to a corner of the field. 'If you'll get in, I'll get clearance.'

He was gone for twenty minutes or so, which gave her time to sort out the chaotic thoughts seething in her head. They were almost swamped by the one overriding all the others: that she loved him and as far as she could see there was nothing to be done about it. He didn't like her, and what was more he was on the point of marrying the awful Christabel; worse than that, she had expressed a wish never to see him again, and if he hadn't needed her because of his mother's illness that would have been the case. She felt the beginnings of a headache just thinking about it. Better not to think.

Presently Haso returned, got into the plane, asked her if she was all right in the same expressionless voice, saw to her seat-belt and started the engine. Suppose she had said that she wasn't all right, Prudence wondered idly, would he have allowed her to get out and go back to Aunt Maud's? She thought not.

When they were airborne she ventured a glance at his profile. It was stern and gave away nothing of his feelings. She gazed lovingly at it and then looked away as he turned his head. 'It will save time if I tell you about my mother. It should take us about three hours to reach Kollumwoude. You will get my mother's room ready for her—everything we might need will be there. I shall go

straight to Leeuwarden, and if it's possible bring her back
by ambulance. Now, the case history...'

The onset had been sudden, although it seemed that
his mother had had a dull, niggling pain for some weeks
and had said nothing about it. Haso had been in
Amsterdam, operating, when he had had a message from
the faithful Wigge, and by the time he had driven himself
back home his mother was in great pain and Wigge had
most sensibly sent for a colleague of Haso's, who had
diagnosed appendicitis and arranged for his mother to
be taken at once to Leeuwarden Hospital. But before
they could operate the appendix had burst and she had
developed peritonitis. 'She had surgery, antibiotics and
drainage,' went on Haso in a voice rigid with control.
'She has been very brave but she is exhausted. You have
to give her the heart and strength to recover, Prudence.'

Prudence thought of Mevrouw ter Brons Huizinga, so
happy in her garden, so kind, and the least deserving of
such a catastrophe.

'I'll get her well again,' she promised.

'Thank you! Now, this we will do for her treatment...'
Haso detailed it calmly, just as though he had been on
a ward round discussing any one of his patients.
Prudence listened quietly, interrupting only when she
wasn't quite sure about something, and by the time he
had made everything clear they were nearing Leeuwarden
airfield. Haso began his descent. 'I told Wigge to leave
the car here. We'll go straight home.'

He taxied into a corner of the airfield, helped her out
of the plane, fetched her case and started towards the
airport. It was quite small and not busy; within fifteen
minutes they were free to leave and go to the car park.
The Daimler was there; Prudence would have been sur-

prised if it hadn't been, knowing Haso. She got in beside him without a word and sat silently going over in her mind all the things she would need to do when they arrived.

Wigge was at the door when they arrived. He ushered her in with a welcoming smile and said something to Haso.

'My mother is holding her own. I doubt if she'll be fit to move until tomorrow. I'm going to the hospital now. You will stay here, Prudence, and see that everything is ready for her. Wigge will look after you.'

Upon which somewhat high-handed remark he went back to the car and drove swiftly away. Prudence stood in the hall, looking at the door through which he had gone, wanting to comfort him, to dispel the stony calm of his face.

Wigge patted her on the arm and gave her a comforting smile, picked up her bag and led the way upstairs. There were several doors opening on to the gallery and corridors on either side, one leading to another small staircase, the other to the wing to one side of the house. Wigge opened the door to one side of the staircase and ushered her inside, put down the case and beckoned her to go through a door on the opposite side of the room. The bathroom they passed through had everything that a woman could wish for, but Prudence was given no time to look around it. Another door led to a large room which had been cleared of all but the most essential furniture. There was a hospital bed against one wall, a small desk at the window, two small easy chairs ranged against one wall, a drip stand, a small trolley and a plain table with a cloth. Prudence reflected that once her patient was installed a few flowers wouldn't come amiss, and a

prettily shaded lamp or so would help remove the severe
hospital aspect. But Wigge was still walking ahead of
her, to open another door—another bathroom, well
stocked with everything she would need for Mevrouw
ter Brons Huizinga. She made her approval felt and went
back to her room.

'*Koffie?*' Wigge beamed at her and, when she nodded,
said, '*In Eetkamer?*' And at her second nod he made
his stately way downstairs.

The room was charming and held every comfort, its
cream walls a splendid background for the peach and
grey brocade of the curtains and quilted bedspread.
Prudence's feet sank into the cream carpeting as she inspected the mahogany bed, the tallboy, the table and
triple mirror between the two long windows. There were
even one or two English novels on one of the bedside
tables. And flowers—little bowls beautifully arranged.
Someone, she had no idea who, had taken care to see
that she should feel welcome.

She would have liked tea, but the delicious coffee was
welcome, accompanied by small sweet biscuits. She felt
hollow inside and hoped there would be a more substantial meal later. She was polishing off the last of the
biscuits when the telephone rang and Wigge came, soft-
footed, to answer it.

It was Haso. 'My mother is holding her own very well;
she will be brought back home tomorrow afternoon—
be ready for her then. You have all you want? Do ask
Wigge for anything you need—his English is sparse, but
he understands simple words. Be kind enough to ring
Aunt Emma and tell her that my mother will be home
tomorrow, but may see no visitors.' There was a short
silence. 'Goodbye for the moment, Prudence.'

She hadn't had a chance to say a word. She hung up and went to unpack and hang up her few clothes, and found that someone had laid several white overalls on the bed. What was more, they fitted her.

Downstairs again, she telephoned Aunt Emma, a lengthy business, as Aunt Beatrix had to have her say as well; she passed on Haso's message, listened patiently to the two ladies' agitated replies, interlarded as they were with their own symptoms and uneasy anxiety, spent several minutes reassuring them as to their state of health, and rang off, promising to let them know any further news.

It was heartening to find Wigge at her elbow with a glass of sherry on a tray, and to make out, from his splintered English, that dinner would be served within a very short time.

Prudence drank her sherry, remembered that Aunt Maud had to be rung and had a brief conversation with her, and, bidden by Wigge, crossed the hall to the dining-room. It had been difficult to examine it thoroughly when she had lunched there with Mevrouw ter Brons Huizinga and Sebeltsje. Now she had the leisure to do so as she sampled the vichyssoise soup, the poulet chasseur with its accompanying dish of tiny young vegetables, followed by crème soufflé à l'orange, washed down by a white wine served by Wigge. It was a large room with an ornamental plaster ceiling, panelled walls, and furnished with a vast sideboard with a good deal of marquetry, an oblong table of some size with chairs in the Chippendale style, and a long case clock also covered in marquetry, and all of them in mahogany. There were a great many paintings on the walls, but those she decided she would examine at close quarters at some later date.

It was a beautiful room, cleverly lighted with wall sconces and a delicate chandelier, and the velvet holly-red curtains gave it warmth. She drank her coffee at the table, wished Wigge goodnight and went up to her room, to lie in a hot bath, extravagantly laced with bath essence, wondering what the next day would hold for her.

It held a great deal—the morning, spent in a leisurely inspection of the garden, the answering of various telephone calls from members of the family, coffee taken on the veranda, gave her no indication of the rest of the day's activities. After a delicious lunch she had gone to her patient's room, made sure that everything was in readiness for her return and then changed into one of the overalls. There had been no messages, so presumably Mevrouw ter Brons Huizinga was considered well enough to return to her own home. Prudence went over the essential details of her illness, given so succinctly by Haso, and then sat down to wait. It was another lovely day. She settled herself by the window and looked out on to the gardens and thought about Haso.

Haso arrived first, bade her an impersonal good day, asked her if she had everything she needed, went away to talk to Wigge and the cook, and was back in the hall where Prudence was waiting. 'Better if you are already in her room,' he suggested, so she went obediently back upstairs.

His calm, cool manner towards her was to set the pattern of their relationship, she supposed, and indeed it would be the best, for they would have to meet and talk in a professional capacity for the next few weeks. Somehow, she would have to learn to hide her own feelings and present a similar manner towards him.

The ambulance arrived, and Mevrouw ter Brons Huizinga was borne upstairs and laid gently in her bed, with Haso standing in the background, not interfering, but letting Prudence oversee this delicate operation and then make her patient comfortable. She was appalled at the wan features, the sunken eyes and weary lines on Mevrouw ter Brons Huizinga's face. She was indeed, it seemed, very ill, and just for a moment Prudence wondered if Haso had been wise to allow his mother to return home, but then she opened her eyes and looked straight at Prudence. 'Just what I have wished for,' she whispered. 'Now I shall get better—home and Haso, and you, my dear.'

Prudence murmured soothingly and set about connecting up the drip ready for Haso to insert it; it was only the fourth day after her operation, and so far her patient was barely holding her own. It was going to be an uphill fight, but Haso's mother, unless she was very much mistaken, was a strong-willed and determined person; if she set her mind to getting well again, she would, only it was going to need a lot of help from all concerned.

The rest of the day was taken up with numerous nursing duties which she carried out meticulously. There would be another nurse, of course, but Mevrouw ter Brons Huizinga had begged her to stay as evening turned into night, so the two of them had done what was necessary and Zuster Helsma, a cosy, middle-aged woman with, thank goodness, a working knowledge of English, had gone to her room to sleep and return to duty in the early hours of the morning when Prudence would take time off and return to take over again later in the morning.

The household had been well organised. She had gone to her dinner while Haso sat with his mother, and around midnight Wigge trod silently from the kitchen and tapped gently at the door. When she opened it, he indicated a tray of coffee and sandwiches on the table outside, and went just as silently away again. The old house was quite quiet, but Prudence sensed that a good many of its occupants were awake. Haso came from time to time, professed himself satisfied, cast an eye over Prudence's neat charts, told her in the calm, flat voice she had begun to dislike that should she need him he would sleep in the adjoining dressing-room, and that he was to be called immediately she felt it necessary. He assured her that a routine would be worked out in the morning so that she and Zuster Helsma had their share of off duty, and then he went away again.

Mevrouw ter Brons Huizinga woke from time to time, was made comfortable and slept again, while Prudence kept her quiet vigil by the bed, checking pulse and drip and blood pressure; she was very tired by now. At intervals Haso came in, and at three o'clock, when Zuster Helsma took over, he injected a sedative, pronounced his satisfaction as to his mother's condition and went away.

Prudence, sinking fathoms deep into sleep shortly afterwards, barely had time to wonder if he was sleeping too. She doubted it.

She was up again soon after seven o'clock, fresh and neat in her white overall, ready to do battle on her patient's behalf. Mevrouw ter Brons Huizinga was showing signs of doing battle for herself; there was a slight improvement as the day wore on, and the bleak chill of Haso's face held a tinge of warmth. Prudence

spent her brief off duty strolling in the gardens with
Prince as escort and, just as on the previous evening,
stayed with her patient until she had fallen into a restful
doze, so that it was in the small hours when she finally
got to bed herself, to sleep the sleep of someone who
had done a good day's work and knew it.

The days went by. Haso had his work, but every
minute he could spare he spent with his mother, and the
improvement by now was marked. She was able to take
fluids now, and each morning she was lifted from her
bed and sat in a chair by the window, well wrapped up
while her bed was made. She was a shadow of her former
self, but at least the shadow was beginning to have
substance.

For the first time, she was allowed visitors—Aunt
Emma and Aunt Beatrix. Prudence, ushering them into
the bedroom, warned them that five minutes was to be
the limit, and indeed ushered them out again exactly on
time, much to their surprise. 'Really, dear,' observed
Aunt Emma, 'surely my own sister-in-law... you are remarkably severe.'

Prudence eyed the two ladies tiredly. 'I'm sorry, but
Mevrouw ter Brons Huizinga is still very weak. Next
time, perhaps a little longer.'

'Well, of course, dear, you know best, I dare say. Poor
dear Cordelia...' She looked at Prudence. 'You look a
little peaked, child. You should get out more.'

Two days later there was another visitor—Christabel,
a cool, chic vision in white, laden with grapes and hot-
house flowers and a pile of magazines.

She greeted Prudence in the hall, where Wigge had
prudently asked her to wait. 'I must say Wigge forgets
himself, leaving me standing here. I've come to see

Mevrouw ter Brons Huizinga.' Her hostile gaze swept over Prudence's severe uniform. 'You're her nurse, I suppose. I'll go up myself now.'

'She's sleeping and still ill. Perhaps you'll come again in a few days' time. I couldn't possibly wake her.'

'Nonsense! She will be delighted to see me. I dare say she needs cheering up.'

'Not while she's asleep,' pointed out Prudence. 'So sorry...'

Suddenly Christabel cast her a look of dislike. 'No wonder Haso's so gloomy these days; he must hate having you in the house!' She thrust the flowers and grapes into Prudence's arms. 'I shall complain to him.'

'You do that,' Prudence, made irritable by lack of sleep and long hours, snapped back. 'I couldn't care less. I'm here as his mother's nurse and I merely obey orders.' She added, 'And you can take these magazines back with you; my patient isn't able to hold anything heavier than a hanky at present. You might have realised that if you'd thought about it.'

They glared angrily at each other before Christabel turned on her heel and walked out to her car. Wigge, appearing from nowhere as usual, closed the door after her, smiled at Prudence and asked in bad English, 'I bring tea?'

'Oh, please.' She went back to her patient, who was awake, sitting up against her pillows, her head turned towards the windows so that she could see the gardens. Prudence gave her a drink and smiled at her. She smiled back and said, 'I feel better—stronger too. Your doing, Prudence.' And when Prudence smiled and shook her head she added, 'If Christabel calls, I do not wish to see her.'

'She came just now. I asked her to come back later.'

'Much later, I think.' Her blue eyes scanned Prudence's face. 'You're tired and Christabel has annoyed you. When will Haso come again?'

'This evening, I believe, *mevrouw*. He had to go to den Haag. Are you too warm? I'll bathe your face and hands, then perhaps you can take a nap?'

Haso came later. He nodded to Prudence, read the charts and sat down by the bed. 'Do go and have dinner, Prudence. When does Zuster Helsma come on duty?'

'Round about midnight.'

She waited a minute to see if he had anything further to say, and when he remained silent, went downstairs to her meal. Wigge was waiting for her in the small breakfast-room behind the drawing-room, the table nicely laid ready to serve the delicious food the cook sent up each day. He poured her a small glass of sherry and offered this to her with a paternal air which she found very comforting. He had taken upon himself the duty of looking after both her and Zuster Helsma, and, although there were servants enough, it was always he who saw to it that they had all they wanted.

Prudence sat alone at the table, carrying on a desultory conversation with Wigge, each of them trying out their very sparse knowledge of the other's language. But she didn't stay long; Haso would be tired after his day's work, and indeed, after a few words he went away, saying as he went through the door, 'If you are not too tired I should like to speak to you when you come off duty, Prudence. I shall be in the study.'

There had hardly been time for him to have seen Christabel, but she had a nasty feeling that that was why he wanted to see her. She dismissed him from her mind

with some difficulty and applied herself to her nursing
duties, and later, when Zuster Helsma took over and
their patient slept, she went downstairs, aware that her
nose shone, her lipstick had long ago vanished and her
hair was a riot of curls, but not caring; Haso wouldn't
notice, and presently she would go to bed.

She knocked and went in and found him sitting behind
his desk, writing. He got up, offered her a chair and said
coldly, 'I won't keep you long. I saw Christabel this
evening, for only a few minutes, but she was very upset
at your rudeness this afternoon.'

Prudence turned large eyes to him. 'Was I rude? You
would have wanted me to wake your mother to listen to
Christabel's silly chatter when she was enjoying a re-
freshing sleep?' She saw his eyes flash and added, the
bit between her teeth now, 'And do tell her not to bring
any of those glossy magazines—your mother can't possibly hold them. Really, she should have the wit to know
that. Now you can blast me; I'm too tired to listen,
anyway.'

She sat, her hands tidily in her lap, and watched his
face. Poor dear, she thought, he's so tired too. If he had
liked me just a little, we could have talked so comfortably together.

'You have played a major part in saving my mother's
life and she depends on you. I am grateful for all that
you have done, but if it were not for that dependence I
would suggest that you returned home. You are a very
unsettling girl, Prudence. I trust you implicitly as a nurse,
but I'm not sure that I do as a woman. I cannot lose
sight of the fact that it was I who urged you to come
here, very much against your wishes, too. I'm very sorry
for that, but I would do the same again, you know.

However, I cannot have you disrupting my life. Just as soon as my mother is recovered, you are free to go.'

Prudence stood up. 'Well, thanks for nothing!' Just for the moment her love was swallowed by rage. 'Free to go? To a job I haven't got because you cancelled it? I said once that I never wanted to see you again, and I meant it, only you came along, arranging things to suit yourself. Now I'll say it once more, and mean it—my goodness, how I mean it!'

She swept out of the room and up the staircase and into her room, where she flung herself on to the bed and had a good cry. Rage and love and misery, nicely mixed.

CHAPTER EIGHT

BEYOND a rather pale face, Prudence showed no signs of a prolonged weep and an almost sleepless night. She attended to her patient's needs once Zuster Helsma had gone off duty, meanwhile chatting of this and that, which belied the strong feelings churning around inside her. When Haso came to pay his morning visit she wished him good morning calmly, although a little colour crept into her face. He gave her a cool stare as he went in, discussed his mother's progress in a placid voice, and suggested that Zuster Helsma might leave within the next day or so. 'For you sleep well, Mama, do you not? And now that you are walking a little, you will find that you will regain your strength rapidly.' He glanced out of the end window. 'It's a splendid day, would you like to sit in the garden? The stairs will be excellent exercise for you. Also, Sebeltsje is quite well again after her cold; she will be coming to see you. Rina and Tialda are coming tomorrow. They were at the hospital with you, but I don't expect you remember that.'

'How nice, dear. They're not bringing the children?'

'No, my dear. Perhaps next week, and not all at once. And you are to say if you get too tired.' He gave Prudence a cool stare. 'I think that we might dispense with Prudence's kind services in another week.'

'So soon? Just as I am beginning to enjoy her company. But of course, you want to get back to your

160

work, my dear.' She smiled at Prudence. 'I expect you have a job waiting for you.'

Prudence managed a bright smile. 'Well, this hasn't seemed like work; it will seem very strange to be in hospital again.'

Even stranger if she were to find a good job at the drop of a hat. She cast a smouldering look at Haso, and encountered an amused look.

'Since Rina and Tialda will be here with you tomorrow, I should think Prudence might have some long-overdue time to herself. They should be here soon after eleven o'clock, I doubt if they will go again much before four or five o'clock. Consider yourself free to do as you like, Prudence. There is a car if you want to drive anywhere.'

She thanked him politely. She didn't want a car, she wanted to walk, or better still, bike along the narrow roads and enjoy the quiet scenery and the sunny weather. Of course she had had off-duty, shared with Zuster Helsma, but they had taken it in turns when and where they could, and never more than an hour or two at a time. It would be delightful to have hours of time all to herself.

Haso went presently and she set about getting her patient ready for an hour or two in the garden. It was a slow business getting there, but Haso had said that his mother was to use the staircase, and that lady was determined to do so. She had her reward once Prudence had settled her in a comfortable chair under the trees at the side of the vast lawn. The flowerbeds were at their very best, it was pleasantly warm and the birds were singing.

'Now I really do feel better,' declared Mevrouw ter Brons Huizinga, drinking the nourishing milk she detested without a murmur. 'Might we not have lunch out here?'

'Why not?' agreed Prudence, 'Just as long as you tell me when you begin to feel tired. Shall I ask Wigge?'

It entailed a good deal of coming and going by Wigge and the maids, but they were so delighted to see the mistress of the house looking almost herself once more that nothing was too much trouble. Bouillon, jellied chicken, puréed potatoes and a crème caramel were borne from the kitchen and set on a daintily laid table with Wigge hovering over them, anxious that his mistress had everything she most fancied. Mevrouw ter Brons Huizinga, who had been inclined to peck at her food, ate a splendid meal, due, she told Prudence, to being outside in her beloved garden. All the same, she was willing enough to climb the staircase once more and be tucked up again in her bed for a nap, and presently Prudence made her way to the balcony and later made her comfortable there where they had tea together.

A very satisfactory day, thought Prudence, getting into bed later, from the point of view of a nurse, but less so from the point of view of a girl in love with a man who didn't care two pence for her. There was no profit in thinking about that; she turned her thoughts to the pleasant time she would have on the morrow.

It was already warm when she got up in the morning, with a hazy sunshine which dimmed the blue sky. She went along to her patient and was kept busy until Haso's two sisters arrived soon after ten o'clock, and hard on their heels Zuster Helsma. Mevrouw ter Brons Huizinga, escorted into the garden again, introduced her daughters, begged Prudence to go quickly and not lose a minute of her free hours, then settled down to a cosy chat with her

daughters while Zuster Helsma, after a quick priming
from Prudence, poured the coffee. 'I'm to go and return
to my former job at the end of the week,' she told
Prudence, 'and you'll be going a day or two later; the
Professor told me yesterday.' She gave Prudence a
questioning look. 'Are you going back to England?'

'Oh yes, I've got to get a job. Where do you work?'

'I work in Leeuwarden—the Professor borrowed me.
I shall go back to my ward.'

Lucky girl, thought Prudence, getting out of her
overall and into a cotton blouse and a matching skirt.
She didn't waste time in worrying about her future, but
hurried down to the kitchen where she found Wigge and,
after a few false starts, managed to make him understand that she wanted to borrow a bicycle. He nodded
in approval; a bicycle to a Dutchman is a second pair
of legs, and in many ways superior to a car. He went
with her to the garage behind the house and wheeled out
an elderly model which Mevrouw ter Brons Huizinga,
at a much earlier date, had used. It was high in the saddle
and the brakes were on the pedals. Prudence, settled in
the saddle, felt rather as though she were on a throne,
but the machine had been kept in good order. She took
a quick turn round the yard before the garage, waved
to Wigge and pedalled off.

She wasn't at all sure where she was going, so she
stopped to read the first signposts she saw and wished,
too late, that she had asked Wigge for a map. The names
were in Friese as well as Dutch, but that merely rendered
them doubly difficult. Dokkum wasn't too far away, she
knew that, but she wasn't sure in which direction. She
could of course go back to the house and ask Wigge; on
the other hand it might be fun just to bike around and

find her own way. The signpost had three arms. She
chose the one on the left, going, if she had but known
it, away from Dokkum. The road was narrow and made
of bricks, and here and there they had sunk so that she
wobbled a good deal, but the fields on either side were
green and the horizon was wide, with no sign of a village.
Well away from the road she could see farmhouses with
their great barns at their backs, and there was a narrow
canal running beside the road. She could glimpse water
ahead of her, and presently came to a small lake, ringed
with bushes and a line of trees. She got off her bike and
stood looking around her, delighting in the peaceful
scene. There were coots darting between the rushes at
the edge of the lake, and a solitary small boat with a
man fishing. He was too far off to notice her and there
was no one else in sight, nor could she see any signs of
a village. She got on her bike again and pedalled on,
reflecting on the possibilities of lunch at the first café
she came across.

Only there were no cafés, no houses or farms either;
the country on either side of her looked empty save for
cows and the occasional farm horse. She came to a
crossroads, but there was no signpost, so she kept straight
on. The canal had wandered off on its own and the brick
road had become even narrower. Not suitable for cars,
she decided, and probably too unimportant to have
signposts either. But it must lead somewhere...

Apparently not, although she passed a solitary farm-
house and then, just as she was beginning to get worried
as to where she was, she saw a man standing by the side
of the road. A farmer, she guessed, with an ugly-looking
dog beside him, but at least he would know the way to
somewhere. She conjured up her smattering of Dutch,

got off her bike, gave him good day and for lack of suitable words, asked, 'Dokkum?'

She repeated herself as he stared at her, and she wondered if Dokkum had a Friese name as well. But this time he took the pipe out of his mouth and waved an arm in the direction of a lane a few yards farther along. It looked to her eye to be even less likely to be going anywhere than the one she was on, so she asked, 'Dokkum?' once more and pointed to the lane.

The man nodded and she thanked him and got back on to the bike. Perhaps it was a short cut.

It was borne in on her after fifteen minutes or so that, even if the lane went to Dokkum, it was by no means a short cut. She passed a couple of cottages, but if she had seen anyone she knew she would never make herself understood. She cycled on, turning over the odd Dutch phrases in her mind, trying to put together something which would make sense when she next saw someone to ask.

She had been too preoccupied to notice that the hazy sunshine had become overshadowed by clouds, and looking over her shoulder she was dismayed to see that the sky behind her was an ominous black. It had grown very still too, and not a bird was singing. A low growl of thunder broke the quiet, and a drop or two of rain fell heavily. Prudence, who hated storms, looked about her in the hope of seeing a farm or a cottage, but there was neither, so there was nothing for it but to go on.

A louder rumble and then a flash of lightning, followed by a resounding clap of thunder, made it all too certain that she would get soaked to the skin and probably die of fright as well. She hurtled round a bend in the lane, obscured by an enormous tangle of shrubs, and braked wildly at the sight of a cottage at the side of a neat small plot of vegetables. She almost fell off her bike and hurried across to the stout wooden door. There was no knocker, so she thumped urgently, and when the door opened said just as urgently and in English, 'May I come in? Unfortunately I'm lost, and it's raining.'

At that moment there was a vivid flash of lightning, followed by a clap of thunder so resonant that she shot thankfully into the narrow passageway. It was only after the hideous din had died down that it penetrated her deafened ears that she had been answered in English. The speaker was an old man, tall and bent, with a shock of white hair and a formidable nose, and as he stood aside for her to go further into the cottage, Prudence paused. 'You are English?'

'No, no, my dear young lady, a retired schoolmaster. Pray come in and make yourself comfortable until the storm is over.'

'Thank you, you're very kind. You see, I'm lost—a man on the other road——' she waved a vague arm '—pointed to this lane. My Dutch is hopeless—I just asked for Dokkum. But it seems an awful long way...'

'It is, and in the opposite direction.'

'Then why did he point this way?'

'Perhaps because my name is van Dokkum.'

He had opened a door in the narrow passage and she went past him into a small room, with a window at both ends and a door at the side.

'Oh, of course, he thought I'd come to visit you, Mr van Dokkum.'

'And I am delighted that he did. A visitor is something of a rarity.'

He swept a pile of books off a chair and begged her to sit down. 'You must forgive the untidiness, but I like to be able to lay my hands on any book I need without having to search for it.'

Prudence surveyed the chaos around her and wondered how he found anything at all among the dozens of books piled on every available surface.

He saw her startled face and said simply, 'I am writing a book, Miss Makepeace.'

She turned a surprised face to him. 'You know me? I don't remember meeting you...'

'We have never met, but news travels fast in this part of the world. The baker—you know—he calls at Haso's house and his aunt's house, and then he comes to me. He was right too; he said you were the prettiest girl he had seen for a long time.'

Prudence blushed. 'Thank you, *mijnheer*. You have lived in England?'

'For some years, a long time ago. My English has become rusty, I think.'

She shook her head. It wasn't that—pedantic perhaps, and a little old-fashioned. She told him so, pleasantly, liking him very much.

The rain was torrential and the storm, at its height, thundered and raged around the little house, but she was barely aware of it. Her host fetched coffee from the small kitchen beyond the door, and they sat drinking it while they talked as though they had known each other for a lifetime.

Presently the rain eased off and the thunder diminished to a distant mutter. 'If you would tell me which way to go, I'll be on my way,' said Prudence. She glanced uneasily at the *stoelklok*, on the wall. 'I said I would be back about three o'clock.'

'An hour's cycling if you go back the way you came. You will have to go to Dokkum another day. But you cannot go before you have shared my lunch. You will be doing me a kindness, my dear. I see few people and it is delightful to talk to you. Surely another hour would not matter? Besides, you should wait for a little while, the storm may return.'

Another hour surely would not matter, it was already almost two o'clock and she was hungry. She agreed to stay and, since Mijnheer van Dokkum refused help, examined the books overflowing the bookcases.

They lunched off rolls and ham and a bowl of strawberries from his garden, and washed them down with more coffee, talking all the time, so that when Prudence next looked at the clock it was to find that it was already half-past three. An hour's cycling before her too, but she couldn't just get up and go like that. She helped him clear away the dishes and was setting the table to rights once more when the cottage door opened. She had her back to it, and the storm, circling back again, was a continuous rumble, so that she had heard nothing. Haso's casual 'Hello' sent her spinning round to gape at him, her pretty mouth half open.

She said the first thing that entered her head. 'How did you know I was here?'

His voice was bland. 'I asked around.'

'But I didn't see anyone—at least, only a man fishing on the lake and another man with his dog.'

'Both of whom gave me an accurate description of you—a big girl with flaming hair.'

'Well——' began Prudence coldly, to be interrupted by Mijnheer van Dokkum, who came from the kitchen with outstretched hand.

'Haso, how delightful—two visitors in one day...' He cocked an eye at Prudence's pink cheeks. 'Looking for this young lady, were you? She was caught in the storm as well as lost and most happily arrived here. You have not been anxious about her, I hope?'

Haso had shaken hands and stood listening to the older man. 'Prudence is well able to cope with events, *meester*, although a local map might have made things easier for her.'

There was a silky tone in his voice which prompted her to say sharply, 'It wasn't suggested, nor did anyone enquire as to what I intended doing. However, Mijnheer van Dokkum had kindly explained how I can get back, so I'll be on my way.'

'I'm taking you back in the car,' said Haso.

'Thank you, but I have a bicycle, Wigge lent it to me.'

He said patiently, 'Yes, I know. You will come back in the car—someone can fetch the bike later on.'

'But I want to cycle back...'

Mijnheer van Dokkum stood equably between them, enjoying himself. 'There is still coffee in the pot, let us have a cup and settle the matter sensibly.'

He had an air of authority which it would have been hard to ignore. Prudence sat down with her shoulder turned to Haso and looked out of the window. A sudden flash of lightening made her turn her head sharply to encounter Haso's stare. Because it was intolerable to sit there under it, she asked, 'You know Mijnheer van Dokkum?'

'He was headmaster of my school. He is, as you may have gathered, a learned man, and a very old friend.'

Their host came back with three mugs on a tray and sat down at the table. He waited until a resounding clap of thunder had spent itself, then observed, 'It would be foolish to cycle in this weather, my dear. The baker comes tomorrow and he will put it on his roof and leave it at Haso's home as he goes past. It will be quite safe here tonight.' He turned to Haso. 'And how are things at the hospital? Busy, I suppose?'

Haso was leaning against a window-sill, looking placid. 'Yes—it doesn't matter what we do to improve things, there's always a waiting list. It's worse in Amsterdam, of course.'

'You have visited our hospital?' Mijnheer van Dokkum asked courteously, and smiled at Prudence.

'No, I haven't...'

She hesitated and Haso said blandly, 'Prudence has had no opportunity to do so. Her pretty nose has been pressed quite ruthlessly to the grindstone. I dare say, if she wishes, I can arrange for her to go round some of the wards either in Leeuwarden or Groningen.' He crossed his long legs and studied his well-shod feet. 'She will be going back to England very shortly. Mama has made a splendid recovery.'

She had no answer to this, and Mijnheer van Dokkum filled an awkward silence by enquiring after Prince.

'He's in the car. I didn't bring him in—he might make havoc of your papers.'

'Very thoughtful of you.' The old gentleman turned to Prudence. 'You have met Prince, of course?'

She nodded. 'He's gorgeous!' She caught Haso's almost satirical eye and added defiantly, 'I like all dogs.'

Haso put down his mug. 'Shall we go? That book you wanted, *meester*, I'll bring it over at the weekend. And it's time you dined with us again. Mama will be so delighted to see you.'

'I'll look forward to it, Haso.' They shook hands and Prudence, not quite knowing why she did it, kissed the old man on his cheek. 'I'm so glad I met you,' she told him.

He had her hand in both of his. 'And I am looking forward to seeing you again,' he told her with the air of a man who was sure that he would. There was no point in refuting this; she murmured something or other and went outside with Haso, to be hurried across the vegetable plot and into the Daimler, where Prince welcomed her with a good deal of panting and whispered barks. She pulled his ears gently and asked him how he did, then sat silent while Haso drove the Daimler down the lane until an open gate into a field allowed him to turn the car. Mijnheer van Dokkum was standing at his door as they went past his little house, and she waved and smiled. She had enjoyed every minute of his company and, even though the afternoon hadn't been quite up to her expectations, it hadn't held a dull moment.

She stole a glance at Haso, but he looked so stern that she decided not to ask him why he had come looking for her to change her mind as a sudden thought struck her. 'Your Mother isn't...she's all right? But Zuster Helsma is there.'

'Zuster Helsma returned to the hospital a couple of hours ago, there's an outbreak of gastro-enteritis on the children's ward.'

'So that's why you came to look for me!'

His 'No' was decisive. It left her puzzled.

The Daimler made short work of the journey back. Prudence looked out of the window, with Prince breathing heavily down the back of her neck. Haso had no wish to talk, so she kept silent. It was magic sitting beside him, but she was profoundly unhappy as well. She would go home and never see him again. She would have to learn to forget him, although that might be difficult, since Aunt Beatrix would pass on news about him from Holland to Aunt Maud, and it would filter through to her. Especially interesting news such as his marriage to Christabel. She heaved a great sigh, thinking about it, and Haso said sharply, 'What's the matter?'

'Nothing, nothing at all.'

He turned into the drive and stopped before his front door and got out. Prudence was still fumbling with her door when he opened it and then turned away to do the same for Prince. Still without speaking they went into the house, to be met by Wigge. He smiled at Prudence, said something to Haso and went to open the drawing-room doors.

'My mother is still downstairs. She will be interested to hear of your meeting with Mijnheer van Dokkum.'

She went past him into the room—and came to a halt. Mevrouw ter Brons Huizinga was still sitting by the window, and there was someone with her—Christabel.

The girl looked immaculate: creaseless silk dress, not a hair out of place, exquisitely made-up. Prudence, only too aware of her own damp, grubby dress, her tousled hair and shiny nose, went slowly red under Christabel's sneering amusement, but she put up her chin and crossed the room to her patient, who had sat up and exclaimed delightedly, 'There you are, my dear! We were a little worried, but I knew Haso would find you.'

'Yes, I'm sorry that I didn't come back sooner. I didn't know that Zuster Helsma had to return to hospital...'

'Was that the reason Haso gave you?'

Mevrouw ter Brons Huizinga sounded amused and Christabel said loudly, 'What other reason could there be? She's a nurse, isn't she? And it's her duty to be with you.'

Haso had come into the room and was standing before the great fireplace with Prince beside him. He said quietly, 'What a good thing there are those of us who fulfil that duty.'

Christabel looked at him doubtfully. 'I don't understand you, Haso.' She gave a little laugh. 'I must go—there's the van Rijns' dinner party this evening. You're going, Haso? Call for me at half-past seven, will you?'

'Very well.' He glanced at his watch. 'You must excuse me, I have some telephone calls to make.'

He and Prince went away, and Christabel gave a little titter. 'I'll say goodbye, *mevrouw*, what good fortune that I was able to take the place of your nurse for a few hours. We had such a pleasant gossip—we share so many acquaintances, don't we?'

Mevrouw ter Brons Huizinga said quietly, 'Indeed, yes. Goodbye, Christabel.' She gave a gentle sigh as the door closed. 'Come and sit down, dear, and tell me about your afternoon.'

Prudence sat, pushed a few unruly curls back from her forehead and gave an account of her adventures. 'I liked Mijnheer van Dokkum,' she finished. 'Isn't he lonely, living in that little house by himself?'

'I should imagine that, writing the profoundly clever books he is engaged on, he might prefer to be alone.'

'But surely someone must do the housework and cook? And what about typing his script?'

'Oh, Haso arranged for someone in the village to go once a week and put clean sheets on the bed and tidy up, and as for the typing, he collects each chapter as it is written and takes it to Leeuwarden to be typed.' Mevrouw added unexpectedly, 'Was Haso very angry?'

Prudence's charming face pinkened. 'I—well, yes, I think so, but he... It's rather difficult to tell, isn't it? I'm sorry I went so far and got lost; it was silly to go out without a map and I didn't notice the time.' She looked anxiously at her companion. 'You were all right? Did Zuster Helsma have to go soon after I went?'

'About an hour, dear. But I had Rina and Tialda. They would have stayed, but Christabel came to see me.' And, at Prudence's look of enquiry, 'They dislike each other— so unfortunate! I was only glad that Sebeltsje wasn't here. She is apt to speak her mind; her sisters are more re-strained. You see, they try to like Christabel for Haso's sake, but of course Sebeltsje has no such idea. She has told him several times that he is making the mistake of a lifetime if he should marry her. I have told her many times that she has no need to worry about that, but she is devoted to him and wishes only for his happiness.'

'She doesn't think Christabel would make him a good wife?'

'And you, what do you think, Prudence?'

Prudence took a long while to answer. She said after much thought and carefully, 'Well, it's hardly for me to say, Mevrouw ter Brons Huizinga,' and then was ap-palled to hear herself say, 'No, of course she's not the wife for him; she's vain and selfish and she doesn't love him, not the kind of love that will wait up for him when he's late home and see that he's fed and cared for when he's dog-tired, and look after his house and see that it's run as he likes it to be, and listen to him when he wants to talk, and not fuss about her clothes all the time...' She stopped, aghast, and saw that his mother was smiling at her.

'You have put it—how do you say?—in a nutshell. One may not interfere, however much one wishes to, one can but hope for the best.'

Prudence stammered a little. 'I'm sorry, I shouldn't have spoken like that, it isn't my business. Perhaps he sees something in Christabel that we can't...'

His mother nodded. 'Oh, yes, dear—or rather, he didn't see it quite as quickly or clearly as we did.' She smiled. 'What a relief!' she observed. 'You know, dear, I think I'd like to go to bed and have my supper sent up. I feel specially well, but I have a great deal of thinking to do.'

So Prudence dined alone, with Wigge hovering attentively. There was no sign of Haso; he would have gone to his dinner party by now and she would be in bed long before he returned. Tomorrow, she promised herself, she would ask him when he wanted her to leave, and arrange her flight back to England. The sooner she was away, the better. She wished Wigge goodnight, paid a brief visit to her patient and, since there was nothing to prevent her doing so, decided to go to bed with a book.

She had bathed and was sitting in her dressing-gown, brushing her hair, when Sieke brought a message. Mevrouw wondered if Miss would very much mind reading to her for half an hour; her brain was too active for sleep and something soothing, read aloud, might quieten it.

It took Prudence a minute or two to understand what was wanted of her. Her Dutch was coming along nicely, although she found speaking the language difficult, but Sieke was adept at sign language and Prudence picked out the essentials, put down her hairbrush and went along to Mevrouw ter Brons Huizinga's room. That lady was sitting up in her bed, looking pleased with herself.

'You don't mind, dear? Something tranquil? *Pride and Prejudice* perhaps... I have always enjoyed that bit where Mr Darcy refuses to dance with Elizabeth.'

'Oh, right at the beginning—shall I read it to you now?'

Prudence went to the little bookcase in a corner of the room, found the book and settled down to read. She had read for ten minutes or so when her companion observed, 'They are very alike—Christabel and Miss Bingley.'

Prudence stopped reading. 'Well, yes, I think perhaps they are...'

'Miss Bingley didn't get Mr Darcy, though, and nor will Christabel get Haso,' went on Mevrouw ter Brons Huizinga with relish. 'They both made the same mistake—they didn't know their man.'

She looked at Prudence, expecting an answer. 'Well,' said Prudence slowly, quite forgetting that she was talking to Haso's mother, 'he can be very tiresome, you know—that bland face—one never quite knows what he's thinking, and he has quite a nasty temper, he needs someone to dilute him. But he's utterly dependable, isn't he? And kind...' She amended this, 'Well, kind to the people he likes and loves.'

'He has been unkind to you, my dear?'

'Oh, no. Just overbearing and dictatorial and impatient...' Reason had taken over her wandering thoughts. 'Oh, good heavens, what have I been saying? I—I do beg your pardon, *mevrouw*, I must have almost lost my wits—please forget what I said. It was unpardonable of me. Haso's your son and he is devoted to you, and I had no right to criticise him.'

Her patient appeared quite unshaken. 'Yes, dear, I know he is, but I think that of all the people he knows, you have the most right to criticise him.'

Prudence decided not to think about that. She said hastily, 'Shall I go on reading?'

Just in time; Mr Darcy and Elizabeth Bennett were crossing swords in the ballroom when she heard a faint sound behind her and turned her head to see Haso standing in the doorway.

He strolled into the room and she stood up, closed the book and put it back on the shelf and edged towards the door. But his genial, 'Don't go, Prudence,' brought her to a halt. 'Can you not sleep, Mama? Would you like a little something to help—a sleeping pill?' He looked at Prudence, taking his time about it. 'Although I should imagine that Prudence is a better alternative.'

Indeed she looked quite beautiful, with her hair in a bright tangle of curls and the dressing-gown Pretty disapproved of doing very little more than enhancing her splendid figure.

It annoyed her very much that she was blushing, but she looked away from his bright stare and addressed herself to Mevrouw ter Brons Huizinga.

'You're quite comfy? There's nothing more that you need? Then I'll go to bed, *mevrouw*. If you need anything later on, you'll ring?'

She went to the door. 'Goodnight, *mevrouw*, goodnight.' The second goodnight she addressed with a distinct cooling of tone to Haso, and his firm mouth twitched, although his own goodnight was casual. She went through the door in a hurry, forgetting to shut it behind her, and she went to her room, where she brushed her hair once more, stared for a long time at her reflection in the looking-glass, went over—word for word—what Haso had said, which wasn't much, she had to admit, and went to bed.

Just as she was on the verge of sleep, she shot upright against her pillows. She had forgotten to tell the cook that her patient had expressed a desire for a coddled egg for breakfast in place of the usual scrambled egg, sent up without question each day. She got out of bed, put on her dressing-gown once more, and found a pencil and some paper. Her Dutch conversation was scanty, but she could pen a simple message as long as the reader wasn't fussy about the grammar. With her note in her hand, she opened her door and crossed the landing to the staircase. Mevrouw ter Brons Huizinga's door was ajar. Her patient's voice was soft but very clear; moreover, she was speaking English, and Prudence could hear her very plainly.

'Such a dear girl,' declared her patient. 'I can never repay her for her care and kindness.'

Prudence had been well brought up; one didn't listen to other people's conversation, and anyway, listeners never heard any good of themselves. She did her best to turn a deaf ear and put a foot on the first step, but she couldn't help hearing Mevrouw ter Brons Huizinga's voice, although the only word she could distinguish was 'Christabel' uttered urgently, to be followed by Haso's decisive voice, 'Of course I intend to marry her, Mama.'

She took another reluctant step, shamelessly listening now, but quite unable to hear what his mother was saying. However, she couldn't fail to hear every word Haso said in reply, 'Love her? Marry her?' He laughed, but he didn't sound amused. 'She's only looking for a wealthy husband and a lazy, empty life. Oh, I know I brought her here and for a time I suppose I found her amusing... There was someone else before we met.' Walter, thought Prudence.

He must be moving round the room, she decided dully, for his voice had become a murmur. She stood very still, going over every word he had said: each one of them hurt like a knife wound and she felt hot and cold at the shameful thought that Haso looked upon her as a scheming woman. She had become resigned to his dislike, but all the time he had despised her...

His voice, suddenly nearer, sent her scuttling soundlessly back to the gallery, but not before she heard him say, 'It's a pity I must be in Amsterdam tomorrow and won't be able to see her—I'll do so as soon as I come back.'

He would see her if he came through the door. Prudence slid silently into her room and closed its door, to stand with her back to it; listening, she heard Haso bidding his mother goodnight and then his footsteps going down the staircase.

For the moment rage was uppermost in her mind, and a strong wish never to see him again. Unhappiness would come presently—but before she gave way to that she must make plans.

CHAPTER NINE

TO GET away as quickly as possible was more important than anything else. To do it without calling forth a lot of enquiries, Prudence would need an urgent summons from Aunt Maud. If she received it the following morning, she would be away by the evening. How fortunate that Sebeltsje was coming to spend a few days with her mother and could take her place. Mevrouw ter Brons Huizinga no longer needed a nurse; her maid was a sensible woman and there were ample domestic staff. Prudence hated leaving her patient, but there was no reason why she shouldn't. Besides, if she went away, there was a better chance of her patient and Christabel becoming friends.

There was a phone by the bed; she dialled Aunt Maud's number.

Her aunt's voice came very clearly over the wire. 'Prudence? How nice to hear from you, my dear!'

Prudence didn't mince matters. 'Aunt Maud, I have to have your help, only I can't explain now. I want you to telephone me here in the morning, early, and ask if I can come back to England without delay. You can be ill—never mind what, but you need me to nurse you...'

Aunt Maud was no fool. 'You're running away, dear.'

'Yes, but I want to do it nicely and nobody must know. Aunt Beatrix is staying in Holland for another few weeks, so there's no fear of anyone finding out.'

'And you can't tell me why?'

'No, Aunt Maud. Only that I've not done anything wrong; it's just that I have to get away from here very quickly.'

'Ah—you've met someone who's swept you off your feet?'

'Yes. Oh, Aunt Maud, you must help me!' Prudence swallowed back threatening tears. 'Mevrouw ter Brons Huizinga is quite well again, and her daughter will be here to help.'

'And Haso?'

'He's away. He's going to Amsterdam.'

'You want to leave while he's away?' Aunt Maud added quickly, 'I'm not prying, dear, and of course I'll help you. Would pneumonia do, or perhaps a mild stroke?' And, when Prudence didn't answer, 'A stroke sounds more urgent, but then of course I wouldn't be able to telephone to you—a broken leg, I think. I'll phone early in the morning and expect you when I see you. And, Prudence—I'm so sorry!'

Prudence mumbled her thanks, got into bed and after a short bout of weeping fell into a troubled sleep. She awoke early, paid her customary visit to her patient and was almost dressed when Wigge tapped on her door to tell her she was wanted on the telephone. 'A call from England,' he told her in the slow, basic Dutch he used when addressing her, and gave her a look of concern.

It was Aunt Maud, acting her part so well that just for a moment Prudence almost believed she had broken a leg. 'I'll come as soon as I can,' she said for Wigge's benefit, as he was hovering behind her.

That made it easier for her. It wasn't difficult to make him understand that she would have to return to England as soon as possible to look after her aunt. He received the news with a sympathetic shake of the head and an offer to get her a seat on the first available plane. She thanked him warmly, feeling mean, and went to tell her news to Mevrouw ter Brons Huizinga. She felt even meaner doing this, for that lady was instantly all sympathy and full of helpful suggestions. Wigge would drive her to the airport, and had she got enough money, and was there anything she needed to take with her?

Prudence went to finish dressing, feeling like something nasty under a stone. All the same, her plan was working; she would be gone by the time Haso got back. For her peace of mind, it was a good thing that she didn't know he had telephoned while she was getting her patient ready for her breakfast, and Wigge had told him she would be returning to England as soon as a seat could be booked on a flight.

Haso had listened carefully to Wigge and then talked at some length, and Wigge had listened in his turn and then put down the receiver. He thought it all a little puzzling, but it would never have entered his head to do anything but what he had been asked.

Accordingly, he waited until Prudence had settled her patient and then sought her out. There were no seats available, he had tried every available source, but he had booked her on an early morning flight the next day. The ferries, he pointed out in his painstaking mixture of Dutch and English, wouldn't save any time at all; there was no time for her to catch the day boat, and the night boat, coupled with the train in England, would get her back several hours later than the early morning flight.

She agreed reluctantly, comforting herself by the thought that Haso wasn't due to return until the following evening anyway. She would be back home by then. She thanked Wigge and went away to tell Mevrouw ter Brons Huizinga and accompany her to the garden, where they were presently joined by Sebeltsje and Prince.

The day, from Prudence's point of view, dragged; she packed the cases, counted her money and went with Sebeltsje and Prince for a walk in the grounds, to find when they returned that Christabel was there, sitting by Mevrouw ter Brons Huizinga, regaling her with an account of a concert she had been to on the previous evening. Her companion, too polite to show boredom, none the less looked glassy-eyed, and Prudence made haste to suggest tea while Sebeltsje exclaimed, 'Oh,' and then in Dutch, 'You here again? Haso is away.'

Prudence did not wait to hear Christabel's reply, but went to find Wigge, and when she got back Christabel was asking her hostess how much longer she would need her nurse.

Mevrouw ter Brons Huizinga spoke in English. 'Prudence goes home tomorrow. Her aunt in England is ill and needs her. We shall all miss her.'

'You won't be able to say goodbye to Haso,' observed Christabel with satisfaction. 'But then, of course, you really don't need to—you're only the nurse.'

This unforgivable remark was met with a stony stare from her three companions, and an icy silence broken by Sebeltsje's outraged voice, 'What a very nasty remark to make—but then you always were spiteful. I dare say Haso will go over to England and see Prudence when he gets back.'

Christabel went an angry red. 'What nonsense! Why should he do that?'

'Good manners, Christabel. But you wouldn't know about that, would you?'

Christabel flounced out of her chair. 'I won't stay for tea. It's to be hoped that when I am Haso's wife, we shall achieve a better relationship.'

Sebeltsje opened her eyes wide. 'Never tell me he has proposed . . . ?'

Christabel opened her handbag, inspected the contents and said carefully, 'He will do so.' She closed the bag and glared at Sebeltsje. 'I will say goodbye.' She shook Mevrouw ter Brons Huizinga's hand, ignored Prudence and with a brief *'Tot ziens'* to Sebeltsje, walked away.

No one spoke until they heard the car drive off.

'Tiresome girl,' observed Mevrouw ter Brons Huizinga.

Her daughter asked anxiously, 'Do you suppose Haso has asked her to marry him?'

'My dear, how would I know?' she replied. 'In any case, there is nothing we can do about it.'

A remark which made Prudence long for the next day, so that she might go away and never come back again, never see or hear of Haso again as long as she lived.

Mevrouw ter Brons Huizinga declared that she was tired after dinner, and when Prudence had seen her safely into her bed, she and Sebeltsje decided to go to bed too. Prudence was to go early in the morning and she still had a few things to pack. But although she had said she was tired, she loitered around the pretty room for a long time, only to go to bed at last and lie awake, thinking of Haso. When at length she fell into sleep, it seemed only a few minutes before she was wakened.

It was another glorious morning. She dressed quickly, fastened her case and peeped in to see if Mevrouw ter Brons Huizinga was still asleep, and, since there was still ten minutes before she needed to go to breakfast, she trod quietly through the house and made for the gardens. She took the narrow path to the swimming pool and went to sit down on the seat by it. This, she reminded herself, was where she had first met Christabel.

'And I called it a paradise for two,' she told a sparrow waiting hopefully for crumbs.

'How very apt!'

She gave a squeak of surprise as Haso sat down beside her, and Prince flopped down and leant his great head against her. She said foolishly, 'But you're in Amsterdam...'

He ignored that. 'Wigge tells me you have to go home to nurse your aunt. I'll drive you there.'

She looked at him with startled horror, and his blue eyes gleamed with amusement. 'No, no, there's no need, really there isn't. I've got a seat on a morning flight—it will be quicker.'

'On the contrary. We will have breakfast and be away within the hour, drive down to Calais and cross over to England by hovercraft. We should be at your home by tea time. Is your aunt in hospital?'

'Yes—no. There's absolutely no need!' She tried to keep the panic out of her voice.

Haso said silkily, 'But I must insist, Prudence; it's the very least I can do after the care and kindness you have shown to my mother.'

Prudence stared down at Prince's ugly face and wished the ground would open and swallow her. She tried again, 'I would prefer to go alone by plane.'

He got to his feet. 'We'll say no more about it. Come, Wigge will have been getting breakfast ready for us, and then we can be on our way.'

It was now or never. Prudence opened her mouth, confession on the tip of her tongue, but he forestalled her. His brisk, 'Come along, then, Prudence,' drove the half-formed sentences from her head. Haso took her arm and marched her into the house. Wigge was waiting in the hall, even at that early hour shaved and dressed immaculately. He opened the door of the small room behind the dining-room, where Prudence had had her meals during the time her patient had been bedridden, and stood aside, his *'goeden morgen'* uttered with his usual solemnity, but he looked smugly pleased with himself.

Prudence went past him and then stopped suddenly. The room was awash with roses, pink and red, yellow and white, massed in a great bowl in the centre of the table, arranged in huge bouquets in vases wherever there was a place to set them, and the jardinière under the window overflowed with them. Her lovely mouth opened in surprise and her eyes widened. They widened still further when she saw the champagne in its silver bucket on the table.

Haso had shut the door behind him and was leaning against it, watching her. 'Do you remember Cornet Castle?' he asked. 'I asked you why you were not married, and you expressed a wish to be swept off your feet, showered with roses, champagne and diamonds. I have done my best at rather short notice, my dear—my very dear girl.'

He came to stand before her and took her hand in his, and opened his other hand to show her what lay within it. A ring, a glowing and exquisite sapphire surrounded by diamonds in an old-fashioned gold setting. 'And this.' He slipped it onto her finger and caught her hand close again.

Prudence, mouth and eyes wide open again, looked at the ring on her finger and then at Haso's face. The look on it would have satisfied the most doubtful of girls, and her heart raced with sudden excited happiness. All the same, there was a question which had to be answered teetering on her tongue. But she couldn't utter before he spoke.

'I saw you on the stairs. You're a big girl—thank God for that—and light on your feet, but I believe I would hear your footfall a hundred yards away. You heard at least part of the conversation Mama and I were having, but not the whole, and you, being you, jumped to conclusions. It seemed to me that you might do something silly...' His tender smile belied his words. 'I warned Wigge to keep an eye on you. He phoned me the next morning and I told him to delay booking your flight, and came back...'

'Christabel...' Prudence interrupted urgently. 'She said...'

'Believe me, my darling, I have never been in love with her—any talk of that or of marriage was fiction on her part. I knew it, of course, but until I met you I didn't bother to do anything about it. She was an amusing companion, someone to take about while I waited until I met the girl I wanted for a wife. You, my darling girl. I went to see her yesterday—as you no doubt heard. She wants only an easy future and plenty of money. If I know Christabel, she is already spreading her net wide.'

Prudence looked up into his calm face, but it was not so calm, she saw, while excitement bubbled inside her. He was looking at her in that same very satisfying manner. She savoured it for a long moment before asking, 'Your mother...?'

'Loves you—so do my sisters. They can't wait to see us man and wife.'

'Aunt Maud? I phoned her...'

'So did I. My darling silly little goose, how I do love you. Will you marry me?'

Haso had let her hand go at last and taken her in his arms, and even if she had wanted to answer him she had no chance, for he started to kiss her with the air of a man who had waited a long time for something, and now that he had it was in no hurry to give it up.

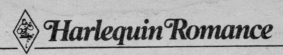
Harlequin Romance

Coming Next Month

#3007   BLUEPRINT FOR LOVE Amanda Clark
Shannon West knows that renovating an old house means
uncovering its hidden strengths. When she meets Griff Marek,
an embittered architect—and former sports celebrity—she
learns that love can do the same thing.

#3008   HEART OF MARBLE Helena Dawson
Cressida knows it's risky taking a job sight unseen, but Sir Piers
Aylward's offer to help him open Clarewood Priory to the
public is too good to miss. Then she discovers that he wants
nothing to do with the planning—or with her.

#3009   TENDER OFFER Peggy Nicholson
Did Clay McCann really think he could cut a path through
Manhattan, seize her father's corporation—and her—without a
fight? Apparently he did! And Rikki wondered what had
happened to the Clay she'd idolized in her teens.

#3010   NO PLACE LIKE HOME Leigh Michaels
Just when Kaye's dreams are within reach—she's engaged to a
kind, gentle man who's wealthy enough to offer real security—
happy-go-lucky Brendan McKenna shows up, insisting that *he's*
the only man who can really bring her dreams to life....

#3011   TO STAY FOREVER Jessica Steele
Kendra travels to Greece without hesitation to answer her
cousin Faye's call for help. And Eugene, Faye's husband, seems
grateful. Not so his associate, Damon Niarkos, the most hateful
man Kendra's ever met. What right does he have to interfere?

#3012   RISE OF AN EAGLE Margaret Way
Morgan's grandfather Edward Hartland had always encouraged
the enmity between her and Tyson—yet in his will he divided
the Hartland empire between them. Enraged, Morgan tries to
convince Ty that he's a usurper in her home!

Available in October wherever paperback books are sold, or
through Harlequin Reader Service:

In the U.S.
901 Fuhrmann Blvd.
P.O. Box 1397
Buffalo, N.Y. 14240-1397

In Canada
P.O. Box 603
Fort Erie, Ontario
L2A 5X3

Janet DAILEY

SWEET PROMISE

Erica made two serious mistakes in Mexico. One was taking
Rafael de la Torres for a gigolo, the other was assuming
that the scandal of marrying him would get her father's
attention. Her father wasn't interested, and Erica ran
home to Texas the next day, keeping her marriage a secret.
She knew she'd have to find Rafael someday to get a
divorce, but she didn't expect to run into him at a party—
and she was amazed to discover that her ''gigolo'' was the
head of a powerful family, and deeply in love with her....

Watch for this bestselling Janet Dailey favorite, coming in
October from Harlequin.

You'll flip . . . your pages won't!
Read paperbacks *hands-free* with

Book Mate • I

The perfect "mate" for all your romance paperbacks

**Traveling • Vacationing • At Work • In Bed • Studying
• Cooking • Eating**

Perfect size for
all standard
paperbacks,
this wonderful
invention
makes reading
a pure pleasure!
Ingenious
design holds
paperback
books OPEN
and FLAT so
even wind can't
ruffle pages —
leaves your
hands free to do
other things.
Reinforced,
wipe-clean vinyl-
covered holder flexes to let you
turn pages without undoing the
strap . . . supports paperbacks so
well, they have the strength of
hardcovers!

Pages turn WITHOUT
opening the strap

SEE-THROUGH STRAP

Reinforced back stays flat

Built in bookmark

BOOK MARK

BACK COVER
HOLDING STRIP

10 x 7¼ opened
Snaps closed for easy carrying, too

Available now. Send your name, address, and zip code, along with a check or
money order for just $5.95 + .75¢ for postage & handling (for a total of $6.70)
payable to Reader Service to:

Reader Service
Bookmate Offer
901 Fuhrmann Blvd.
P.O. Box 1396
Buffalo, N.Y. 14269-1396

Offer not available in Canada
*New York and Iowa residents add appropriate sales tax.

BM-G